'Postle Jack Tales

'Postle Jack Tales

Gospel Images
in New Appalachian Folktales

by

John H. Barden

PUBLISHING

Copyright:

©2004 USA by John H. Barden

Published May 2004 by:

KiwE Publishing, Ltd.
P.O. Box 28007
Spokane, WA 99228-8007
USA
E-mail: kiwe@kiwepublishing.com
Web Site: http://www.kiwepublishing.com

Library of Congress Control Number: 2004105877

ISBN 1-931195-66-8

Printed in the United States of America

Table of Contents

Stories:

Preface

During Reverend John Barden's all too brief sojourn in the mountains of Eastern Kentucky, one of story-telling's traditional characters intruded upon his consciousness. Reverend Barden's introduction to "Jack" came in visionary moment as he and a friend were headed back to Hazard. Transfixed by a "Jack tale" told by Brandon Smith, Reverend Barden found himself keenly in tune with a very old oral tradition. Scholars before Barden, the likes of which include Richard Chase, Vance Randolph, and Leonard Roberts, were similarly caught up and went on to do extraordinary research.

John Barden did his homework and, in this small volume, has faithfully adhered to some of the key motifs of the Jack tale. For many readers, the lure of the tale focused upon the great array of characters that they would hear about, from royalty to thieves, from characters frustrated with their lives to characters quite secure in who they were and what they knew, from children to wise elders, from those who attend revivals to those who do not. Such characters abound in Barden's prose. They take on a believability that makes reading the stories such a delight.

Another key component of the Jack tale is the character of Jack himself. Listeners quite quickly gather a sense of who Jack is in a particular tale, what he feels, what he believes, and to what he must react. A "Jack" character is much less acted upon than acting. Barden's 'Postle Jack fits within that characterization, and this "Jack" has a clear purpose of what he is about and what he must do. He is rarely uncertain. His thinking is logical and methodical, yet he exudes a passion that manifests itself in the course of each tale. Barden's 'Postle Jack seems a loner, yet he is destined to be much involved within the landscape of Barden's fictional region and very involved in the lives of these characters.

Reverend Barden's "Introduction" reveals how he came to develop these stories as one component of his ministry, and I remember quite vividly the conversations he had with several of us in the middle floor of the First Presbyterian Church as he began to flesh out the task at hand. Reverend Barden has succeeded in taking an old tradition and melding it with the ever-constant need to energize spiritually a congregation. And while I will encourage everyone to read these stories, the true rendition of the "'Postle Jack" tales will occur only when an audience hears Reverend Barden tell one. I have had that pleasure and look forward to hearing them again some day.

Ron Reed
Chair, Division of Heritage and Humanities
Hazard Community and Technical College.

Introduction

These stories came into being as a result of several influences on my life and ministry during my years of serving the First Presbyterian Church of Hazard, Kentucky. The first influence was my desire to discover a way to proclaim the gospel in an authentic and engaging manner for a people and a culture I did not immediately understand. I read and listened and researched religion and faith in Appalachia in general and in eastern Kentucky in particular. I discovered much that was truly amazing, and I developed a deep and lasting affection for the unique faith of Presbyterians in the mountains of Kentucky. During the same time, as part of my doctoral work in preaching, I spent a week in Chicago listening to John Shea tell stories. Some of these stories were from the great spiritual traditions, and some were from other sources, but all of them touched my soul and called me to listen to stories in a new way.

Back home in Kentucky, I was riding in the car with my two children, my friend Brandon, and his children on our way home from climbing in the mountains around Hazard. Brandon began to tell a story which captivated everybody in the car. It was a Jack Tale. I soon came to discover there was an entire cycle of Jack Tales, old Appalachian folktales which originated in western North Carolina and spread north to Tennessee, Kentucky, and Virginia. They were collected in the early part of the twentieth century by Richard Chase and others.

I found a copy of Chase's *Jack Tales*, (which includes a wonderful appendix about Jack Tales and the literary criticism which developed as they were collected) and I began reading them to my children. I even shared one with colleagues in the doctoral program in Chicago. They liked the story but they objected to the violent worldview that it projected, and they asked, "Couldn't you just rewrite it and leave that part out?" Well, no, I thought, I couldn't; the worldview of nineteenth-century Appalachia was fairly Hobbesian: "Life is nasty, brutish, and short."

Their query stuck with me, though, and I began to explore what it would be like to write new Appalachian folktales, in the style of the Jack Tales, with a central character like Jack, and characters like the ones he meets. These new stories would echo the parables of Matthew's gospel, and I would tell them in worship. They would present a worldview that intentionally invited people into the ethos of the gospels and spoke of a vision of God's reign of justice, grace, and mercy. I gathered together a group of people from my congregation, and we set out to explore the possibility.

The first three 'Postle Jack Tales were written this way, as reinterpretations of parables from Matthew's gospel, to be told as part of a sermon in worship among the congregation of First Presbyterian Church, Hazard, Kentucky. I anticipated that people would recognize that these were modeled on Jack Tales of a bygone era and they would appreciate my efforts to "speak the native language." What I could not have anticipated was the way these stories would become the congregation's stories, a common language, a common story cycle with which the members of the congregation would shape their worldview and explore their faith. When the first three stories were finished, I wrote one more, just for fun. Then I thought I was finished with the experiment.

The congregation demanded more. I wrote three more and told five of the now seven stories at the local church camp. In the fall, for the stewardship campaign, I wrote another one. I was asked to preach for a Presbytery meeting, honoring the Year of the Child, so I wrote another one. Now I had nine 'Postle Jack Tales, and again, I thought I was finished. I moved to Missouri and I assumed these Appalachian folktales would not be appreciated, but the congregation insisted on hearing them. I soon discovered that many people in this small Midwestern town had ancestors from the mountains of Kentucky and North Carolina and from the Ozarks of southern Missouri and northern Arkansas. I was invited back to the summer camp in Kentucky to tell more stories, and since I had already told five of the nine, I needed a tenth story. The rest of the stories in this collection were written for special occasions: two for the congregation here in Missouri, one for a summer camp in Colorado, and one for a friend's wedding (you can probably tell which is which).

Each 'Postle Jack Tale in this collection was written in dialogue with a particular scripture passage. The scripture is briefly referenced at the beginning of each story. The complete passages of scripture and brief reflections can be found at the end of this volume in a section titled "For further reflection." I have quoted from the New Revised Standard Version of the Bible throughout this work. It is my intention that these stories and these scriptures will be read in dialogue with one another, each interpreting the other and offering insight beyond what I have written on the page. The reflective piece is simply meant to be suggestive, a starting point for your own reflections and interpretations or discussions with others.

I am aware that the use of some language, especially including a character such as the King in these stories, carries with it connotations of monarchialism, patriarchalism, and mysogyny, not to mention the systematic oppression and marginalization of the poor and powerless of all societies throughout the centuries. I made an intentional decision to retain this title and this language in these stories for several reasons. First, "Kingdom of God" language is familiar to the congregations in which I have told these stories, and it is a phrase which is used repeatedly in the common Bible translations from which many people read, so the phrase cannot be ignored. Second, the issues of oppression, marginalization, and patriarchalism are deeply rooted in the cultural experience of the people of Central Appalachia, and as such they are an integral part of the worldview of the original Jack Tales. Third, the original Jack Tales have as a major character in the cycle of stories a king who represents all sorts of socioeconomic issues. It is my hope that these stories will contribute to the ongoing discussion and reinterpretation of the Biblical image of the Kingdom of God for people of faith.

I want to thank Kathryn Green Barden for her encouragement during the writing process of these stories. She has often made a suggestion about adding a character or redirecting a plot line when I was dissatisfied with a particular story or element. She also helped many groups explore these stories through related art activities, discussions, and kinesthetic engagement. I also want to thank my editor, Nancy Hadfield, for bringing a fresh unbiased perspective to her task and for helping to shape the final format of this book.

I have now told these 'Postle Jack Tales in settings in Kentucky, Missouri, Texas, and Colorado. They have also been read, in a slightly different form, by a doctoral thesis review board in Chicago, which granted them an award; you can find a copy in the library of McCormick Theological Seminary, if you are interested in the sociological and theological underpinnings of these stories. It seems that people all over the country enjoy hearing stories, and these 'Postle Jack Tales seem to speak to their hearts in a way other stories don't always try to do. I hope these stories will both entertain and inspire those who read them and those who hear them.

John H. Barden
Fulton, Missouri
Spring 2004

'Postle Jack Makes a Promise

———⟫●⟪———

Your wife Elizabeth will bear you a son…
You will have joy and gladness,
and many will rejoice at his birth.
Luke 1:13-14

———⟫●⟪———

Now, some of you folk may have heard tell of 'Postle Jack, and some of you mighn't have heard nary a word about him. He's just a feller, just like you and me, excepting he was born in the mountains and raised in the mountains. It's in them mountains where 'Postle Jack wanders and has all his adventures. This here is one of them.

It seems 'Postle Jack came walking into a little village way up at the head of a hollow; it was one of them hollows nobody never took no mind of, leastways not in a whiles. Still, there was a passel of folk living up there and working up there all the same. 'Postle Jack, he walked right into the middle of the town, just like he always does. But there weren't nobody anywheres to be seen. A strange silence hung over the town, like the dark silence of a winter night, though it was bright as anything that day. He tried looking in the window of the bakery, but the baker closed the shutters and locked the door. He tried calling out to a woman on her way home with a basket of vittles, but she just hurried all the faster, until she reached her door and shut it with a loud thunk behind her. So, 'Postle Jack, well, he just set hisself down right in the middle of the town, and he waited. After a while, a worn-looking old man come out of one of the houses, and walked right over to him.

"Stranger," says the old man, "how'd you come by our town? We hain't seen nary a stranger from beyond this holler in, law, years."

"Well," says 'Postle Jack, "I was jes' wanderin' past, and figgered as how I'd stop and set a while."

"You're welcome, too," says the old man.

"Father," says 'Postle Jack, "tell me why it's so silent here in your town."

"Well, stranger," says the old man, "it's all on account o' we have no young'uns. Nary a one. Not one baby has been borned here in this holler for nigh on fifteen year. So's there's nobody to run and play, nobody to delight us and make us laugh, no little voices to sing and yell. So ever'body jes' kinda keeps to theirselves and goes about their business the best they kin."

"I'll bedad," says 'Postle Jack. "I never did hear tell of a town with no young'uns a'tall. No wonder hit's silent as night here."

"That's the reason, stranger," says the old man. "But where's my manners? You're a stranger what's come to set a spell, and here I let you jes' linger in the road. Come into my home and share my fare. Hit's jes' me and my wife, and we're simple folk, but what we got, we'll share with ye."

"I thank ye, Father, and I believe I'll take your offer," says 'Postle Jack to the old man, and he follows him into a simple house at the end of the road.

As soon as ever the old man told his wife they had a guest for supper, she set to work fixing up a feast that would of pleased even the King hisself. She set out soup beans and corn bread, sausage and fried apples, shucky beans and ham, and a fresh-baked rhubarb pie to boot. 'Postle Jack, he set at that table and ate his fill, all the while telling them all about his adventures, until every one of them what was sitting at that table done had their fill of what they was hungering for.

"Thank ye, 'Postle Jack, fer telling us 'bout the places you been and the people you met," says the old woman. "Law, I sure wish our town was like some o' them others you been at. Hit jes' 'bout has me wore out, not never havin' no hope fer us."

"Well, Mother," says 'Postle Jack, "I b'lieve as how a child is gonna be born right here in this town, a special child, right soon. And this young'un is gonna bring hope and laughter and joy back to this holler."

"Law, I hope you're speaking true, 'Postle Jack," says the old man. "Hit would do our hearts good to see a young'un raised here."

"I b'lieve that's jes' what's gonna come to pass, Father," says 'Postle Jack, as he takes his walking stick and heads for the door. "I'm gonna come back one day, and when I do, this town will be full o' sunshine. That's a promise." And with that, 'Postle Jack took off down the road, and headed off around the mountain.

Now, it weren't long before that old couple started wondering just who it was would be having a baby. Word started traveling all through town, about the promise what 'Postle Jack had made, and pretty soon, everybody was waiting and expecting a baby to be born any day, wondering who it would be, who would be the mother and the father. One night, after a particularly long day, the old man came home to find his wife setting at the table, just staring into the air. He set down across from her, took her hand in his and waited for her to speak.

After what seemed a long time, finally she said, "I'm with child. We're gonna have us a young'un. Jes' like he promised." Well, the old man, he didn't know should he laugh or cry, so he done both. Then he looked back at his wife.

"Let's not tell our neighbors, not jes' yet. They'll think we've gone plumb crazy, sure as certain, us bein' so old, and thinkin' we kin have a baby."

So, the old couple agreed to keep their secret, for a while at least.

But the very next morning, they woke to a knocking at their door, early. It was their young cousin. She was just now going on sixteen, seeing as how she was the last young'un born, and she was almost grown herself now. They saw she had been crying, so they brung her in and set her at the table and gave her a glass of warm milk and sugar. After a while, the young girl took a deep breath and looked at the old woman.

"Cousin," she says, "I'm with child. I'm gonna have a young'un, and here I am, without even a husband. I thought I'd die of shame, til I 'membered 'bout that promise what that stranger tol' you a while back. So I came here."

The old woman smiled and told her young cousin about her own baby. "Now there will be two. I wonder which young'un will be the One he promised," she says.

Well, it weren't long before word got out, that old Elizabeth and young Mary were both expecting. The whole town entire began to wonder which baby was the One that 'Postle Jack had promised. And they all began to prepare for these young'uns. When these young'uns were finally born, all the neighbors carried in food and such for the parents, and there were dances and parties and such for several days. And everybody came to see the young'uns and ponder on which was the One what had been promised.

But then, something happened. Another child was born in the town, across the way. And then another. The baker's wife had a daughter and the grocer's wife had twins. A few months went by, and five more babies were born. Now there were twelve young'uns in the town, and everybody was tired as they could be, caring for them babies, but they was happier than they could remember ever being.

The elders of the town got together and talked about what had been happening. "Which young'un is the one what was promised?" they asked the old man what had first heard 'Postle Jack speak it.

"Well," he says, "I reckon any of 'em could be. We won't know til they're all growed."

"Seein' as how we don't know which young'un is the special one what was promised," says one of the elders, "we'll have to raise 'em all like they're special, less'n we miss educatin' the Promised One right well." All the other elders reckoned as how this was what they would have to do, and they set about doing it.

A new schoolhouse was built in the town for the young'uns, so's they could all get the learning they needed, "jes' in case this is the Promised One we're educatin'," the elders said of each child, as they entered the schoolhouse. The houses of every family were fixed up, windows replaced, roofs patched, walls painted, so every young'un had a decent place to live, "jes' in case the Promised One lives here," the elders said as they finished each home. The parents were gathered up and set to learning together all about raising young'uns, seeing as how nobody had raised any in a generation and they needed to know how, best they could, "jes' in case this is the Promised One they're raising," the elders said, as they set and rocked the babies so's the parents could go to their meeting. The elders also found every parent a job of work, and made sure as how they were paid fair, so's they could buy the things they needed to raise their children, "jes' in case this is the Promised One they's kearin fer," the elders said as they handed out a fair day's pay for a fair day's work, with nary a complaint.

Well, about this time, 'Postle Jack happened to wander back into the hollow of a morning. And what he saw was a town filled with hope, and laughter, and joy, a town filled with children, and parents caring for children, and elders appreciating children, a town just glowing in the sunshine.

The old man happened to be passing by right then, and he spied 'Postle Jack just standing in the road, smiling. "Well, Neighbor," says the old man to 'Postle Jack, "you're welcome back. And hit seems what you promised has come to pass. But, tell me, 'Postle Jack, which of our twelve young'uns is the special one you done talked 'bout?"

"Which one o' them young'uns has brung hope, Father?" says 'Postle Jack.

"Well, they all did," he says.

"And which one o' them has brung laughter, Father?" says 'Postle Jack.

"Well, they all bring that, certain," he says.

"And which one o' them has filled any heart with joy, Father?" says 'Postle Jack.

"Each one o' these young'uns fills our heart with joy, sure, Jack," he says.

"Then I reckon each child is special, if'n you believe they are, Father," says 'Postle Jack.

"I reckon you're right there, 'Postle Jack," says the old man. "Thank ye for yer Word o' Promise."

Then, 'Postle Jack, he just turned hisself around and set off down the road, looking to see could he find hisself another adventure. Leastwise, that's what he was doing last time I heard tell of him.

'Postle Jack and the Bean Pickers

———>●●<———

For the kingdom of heaven is like a landowner who went out
early in the morning to hire laborers for his vineyard....
When evening came...he said to them, 'Am I not allowed
to do what I choose with what belongs to me?
Or are you envious because I am generous?
Matthew 20:1, 8, 15

———>●●<———

This is the story about how 'Postle Jack did something what nobody else could have expected to do. It had to do with some no-good fellers what thought they was better than others, and the King, and some beans. This was before 'Postle Jack knew much about the King and his ways, and before the King knew much about 'Postle Jack either, otherwise things might not of happened like they did. This is how they did happen, though, sure as telling.

'Postle Jack was walking through a town when he saw some fellers setting on a bench in front of the courthouse.

"Mornin', fellers," says 'Postle Jack to 'em. "Why are you'uns settin' here on sech a fine day as this?"

"We're looking for us a job of work, Jack," one feller says. "Do you know of any?"

"I sure don't," 'Postle Jack says, "but if'n I run across any, I'll sure give you a holler." Then 'Postle Jack left them boys and went on his way.

Now, a little ways out of town, up the hollow, 'Postle Jack walked past a bean patch. It was planted all up the side of the mountain, and them bean vines were growing big and green, just ripe to be picked, with beans all over them. But there weren't nary a soul in sight. Just then 'Postle Jack spied a fine house a little ways up the hollow, and a man was setting on the porch, staring out at the bean patch.

"Hey, stranger," the man called out to 'Postle Jack. "What's your name?"

"Name's Jack," says 'Postle Jack. "Who're you?"

"Why, Jack, I'm the King," says the King, "and this here's my place you're lookin' at."

"Why ain't you got anybody set to pick them beans?" 'Postle Jack asks the King.

"Well, I was jes' thinkin' 'bout how I needed to get that done today. You looking for yourself some work, Jack?"

"That's a might lot of beans to pick you got there, King," 'Postle Jack says. "But seein' as how it's such a nice day, and I hain't got any plans, I'd be willing to help you out."

"Well, Jack, I'd be might pleased to have your help," says the King, making a plan now to get the best of 'Postle Jack. "I tell you what. You get that entire field picked, ever last bean, by evening, and I'll pay you a bag of money," says the King to 'Postle Jack. "And you can have all the beans you ken carry, too, Jack," the King says, looking at 'Postle Jack's tattered coat with nary a pocket to boot.

"Well," 'Postle Jack replies, "I don't have much call for money, but I reckon I could take your offer."

So, 'Postle Jack set off back down the road, but instead of going into that bean patch, he passed right by it and headed hisself back into town. He found those two fellers setting on the bench and he says to them, "Fellers, I got you a job of work. You two go on up the road a ways to that bean patch up yonder and start pickin' beans. I'll pay you day's pay if'n you pick for me. I'll be along directly."

"Sure, Jack," says the fellers, and off they went and set to picking beans. 'Postle Jack sat himself down on the bench, and figgered he'd just take himself a rest a while, after all that walking. The morning tended to wear on, and two more fellers came walking by.

"Hey, fellers," says 'Postle Jack, "you looking for a job of work?"

"Yes, we are," says one of the fellers.

"Well, go on up the road here, and get to pickin' those beans in that bean patch, yonder," says 'Postle Jack, "and I'll pay you what's fair at the end of the day."

"Sure, Jack," says the fellers, and off they went and set to picking beans with them other two fellers already out there.

It was getting to be lunch time so 'Postle Jack took hisself over to the marketplace to find him something to eat. There was a woman at a table by the road, with the best-smelling pot of soup, and a warm loaf of fresh bread.

"Mother," says 'Postle Jack to the woman, "I'm powerful hungry. If you don't care to give me some of that fine soup and bread, I'd be ever so grateful to ye for it."

"Why sure, honey," says the woman, "You can share my fare 'long as I got any to set out." So she serves him up a big bowl of soup and a thick slice of bread, and 'Postle Jack set to eating his fill. While he was eating, the woman's two sons came up.

"We hain't found no work, today, Mother," says the oldest of the boys.

"Well, you boys run on up the holler and pick beans in that bean patch yonder for me, then," 'Postle Jack says to them.

"Yessir," says the boys, and off they went and set to picking beans. When 'Postle Jack had eaten his fill, he thanked the woman and took his leave. But when he passed by the bench in town, two more fellers were just setting there resting theirselves.

"Why, you fellers look like you hain't done a lick of work all day," 'Postle Jack says to them.

"No, sir. Nobody has hired us to do a work."

"Well, then," says 'Postle Jack, "you get up there in that bean patch yonder. I'll be along directly." So the two fellers set off up the road and set to picking beans with all them other fellers who had been working all day.

It was getting along toward evening when 'Postle Jack came back to the bean patch, and he found ever last bean picked and loaded into the cart for hauling.

"You fellers have worked hard," 'Postle Jack says to them.

"We sure have, now pay us what's fair," they says.

"I'll do just that," says 'Postle Jack. "Now, you'uns go over yonder and wash yourselves in the creek while's I take these beans up to the house and bring you your pay."

"King," hollers 'Postle Jack, when he gets to the house. "I got your bean patch picked clean, and here they are." Well, the King was right upset, seeing as how he had expected to get a hard day's work out of Jack, but not have to pay him nothing if he didn't get the job done total.

"All right," says the King, "here's your bag of money. Now be off with you, Jack."

"What about my beans," says 'Postle Jack. "You said I could have all the beans I ken carry." The King reckoned as how he had said just that. 'Postle Jack reached into that bag and took out every last bit of money and laid it on the ground. Then he filled that bag right up to the top with beans. He scooped up the money in his ragged old hat and hoisted that bag of beans up on his shoulder.

The King laughed and said, "You sure are a smart one, Jack."

When 'Postle Jack got back to the bean patch, them fellers were waiting for him.

"Where's our pay," they says.

"Here it is," says 'Postle Jack, setting down his bag and reaching into his hat full of money. First he gave those two fellers that he saw last a wad of money; it was more money than they ever would have hoped for, for even a full day's work of picking beans. These two smiled and went on their way, plumb amazed at what they had got. Then came the two boys whose momma had give him the lunch; 'Postle Jack gave each of them a wad of money too. And so on, until he got to those first fellers he sent out in the morning. And he gave them a wad of money too; as much as them others got, more than a day's pay. Since his hat was empty, he put it on his head, picked up his bag and started on his way.

Now these two fellers were none too pleased at what they had got. They thought they would have got more seeing as how they had worked all day in the hot sun and them others had come only later, when it was getting along toward evening. Besides, they figgered that bag on 'Postle Jack's back was full of money, and him not even working one lick all day. So them two fellers ran after 'Postle Jack and told him what they thought of what he done to them and how it weren't nowise fair.

"Well," 'Postle Jack replies, "didn't I give you what I said, and more?"

"Yes, you did, Jack, but…"

"And wasn't it my money to give it to them other fellers however which way I chose to give it?" asks 'Postle Jack.

"Yes, it was, Jack, but…"

"Well, then, get on home and be glad with what ye got," 'Postle Jack says to them.

But these fellers still weren't satisfied and they allowed as how they weren't.

"What else do ye want?" asks 'Postle Jack.

Eyeing that bag on 'Postle Jack's shoulder, one feller says, "We'll make you a trade. Our two wads of money for that sack on your back, or else…"

"Or else what?" asks 'Postle Jack.

"Else we'll take it from you by force," says the other feller.

"Okay," says 'Postle Jack, "I'll trade ye for it."

So 'Postle Jack gave them fellers the bag off his shoulder and they gave him two wads of money. Those fellers ran off quick as anything with that bag of beans, just laughing and busting a gut about how they had fooled 'Postle Jack. When they opened that bag and saw all them beans, they just stomped and hollered and cussed.

But 'Postle Jack, he went to the woman's house with the two sons and he gave her those two wads of money, for her kindness to him. That old woman was so beside herself, she packed up two big jars of soup and three loaves of warm bread for 'Postle Jack to take with him on his way, and a jar of rhubarb jam to boot. Then 'Postle Jack left that town and went his way on down the creek toward home. Last time I saw him, that's where he was, and he give me this bean out of his pocket, too.

'Postle Jack at Trouble Creek

—————➤●◄—————

There was a landowner who planted a vineyard....
Then he leased it to tenants and went to another country.
Matthew 21:33

—————➤●◄—————

Did I ever tell you of the time 'Postle Jack went up to Corner Hollow? It was named that on account of it was a hollow in a corner of two mountains, just in the bend of Trouble Creek, so's the only way in or out was up over them mountains or by crossing the creek, and it came by its name honest. This was also way off in the corner of the King's land, so far off that it mostly was forgot about, and nobody much had been there for longer than anybody could remember. Well, one day, when the King was looking over some deeds at the courthouse, he noticed something wrote down about Corner Hollow. The King figured if'n it was his land, and there was folks living there, well, he needed to know a bit more about it. So the King called some of his fellers what did for him and sent them off to Corner Hollow, just in the bend of Trouble Creek, just to see what's what.

Well, them fellers weren't gone for more than a few days when they come hightailing it back to the King. Them fellers told about seeing a high wall made of logs built clear across the mouth of that hollow, from one mountain to the other. They reckoned as how there must of been some folk living back up in that hollow, those what must of put up the wall, but they ain't seen them, on account of they couldn't find nary a way to cross Trouble Creek. There weren't no bridge, not even a swing-bridge, nor not even a ferryboat what could be found to carry them over Trouble Creek. So the King called out some other fellers he knew, what had done for him in the past, big fellers who weren't nowise afraid of getting theirselves wet in a creek. Them fellers headed off to Corner Hollow and it weren't hardly no time at all before they were back on the King's front porch with a tale to tell. They allowed as how they had just barely made it crossing Trouble Creek, only to get right up to that strange wall at the mouth of the hollow, where they was greeted by a whole passel of angry fellers with rocks and guns who chased them back across the creek, and hollered at them to never come back their way, "if'n they know'd what was good for 'em."

Now the King was in a real fix. He had plumb run out of fellers to send up to Corner Hollow, and now he seemed to be at his wit's end. So the King sent out a notice all over his lands that if anybody could reach Corner Hollow for him, he'd give that person a wad of money and a prize to boot.

'Postle Jack heard tell of the fix the King was in, and of the wad of money and a prize to boot that the King was offering. So 'Postle Jack took hisself over to the King's house, walked up onto the porch and commenced to banging on the door. It weren't but a moment before the King hisself was standing at the door.

"King, I hear tell you got yourself in a real fix," says 'Postle Jack.

"Law, 'Postle Jack," says the King, "hit's the worst I seen in I cain't remember when."

"Well, King," says 'Postle Jack, "I think I may be jes' the one to help you."

"I'd be right pleased to have your help, 'Postle Jack, if'n you think you kin."

"Well, now, King, I think I kin be of help, but I need a few things first, if you don't care to give 'em to me."

"Why, no, 'Postle Jack, I don't care a bit to. Take what ever you have a mind to take; what's mine is your'n."

" 'Preciate you, King," says 'Postle Jack, and they shook hands on the deal.

'Postle Jack gathered him up a wagon and a cow to pull it, and he loaded that wagon down with a bucket of gold paint, a sack of coins, a bolt of purple cloth, and a beautiful dulcimer made from cherry wood. It weren't long before 'Postle Jack caught sight of that bend of Trouble Creek and Corner Hollow across the creek, with the strange wall stretched from one side to the other. 'Postle Jack hid the wagon and all his boodle behind some trees a fair piece from the creek. Then he took hisself right to the edge of Trouble Creek and started wading into the water. 'Postle Jack had just stepped out onto the other bank of the creek, and was making for that wall, wondering how he was going to get hisself over the top of it, when a passel of angry fellers stepped in front of him and blocked his way.

"Hey fellers," says 'Postle Jack. "Is this here Corner Holler?"

"It is," says the biggest, meanest-looking feller of the whole bunch. "And if'n you know'd what's best, ye'd be gittin' back cross that creek and not comin' back here, stranger."

"Well, now, friend," 'Postle Jack says, "I cain't do that jes' yet. I've come on the King's bidness. He asked me to bring you fellers some presents."

"The King ain't got nothin' we want," says the same feller. "'Bout a hundred years ago, the Old King brought our people here and set 'em down in this holler, and he promised they'd be livin' in the grandest village of his kingdom. Then he went off and didn't pay us no mind for years and years. We figgered if'n the Old King had no use for us'n, well, we had no use for him. So we built this here wall to keep out that Old King and all other strangers who we ain't got no use for, anyhow. So you best be gittin' on back over t'other side of the creek, stranger."

"Well, I'll go," says 'Postle Jack, "but I cain't leave jes' yet."

"Suit ye'self," says the same feller.

When 'Postle Jack got back to the other side of the creek, he went and found his wagon. Then he took the cow and painted it solid gold. He led that painted cow down to the creek, and there he sat down next to it, and waited. When evening came, 'Postle Jack set to milking that gold cow, and them fellers gathered cross the creek, watching whatever he was doing. 'Postle Jack knew them fellers were spying him, but he just kept on milking.

"This here's one of them presents the King says I'm to give ye'," shouts 'Postle Jack over to the fellers.

"What is it?" asks the feller what spoke earlier, who always seemed to do all the talking.

"This here's one of the King's Golden Cows. Why, he's got a whole herd o' these Golden Cows, and ever one of 'em gives golden coins instead of milk when you set to milking them." 'Postle Jack reached down behind the milk pail where he had laid that sack of coins, and he pulled up a big handful to show them fellers.

"We hain't got much use for gold coins here in Corner Holler," says the main feller, "seeing as how we hain't got nothin' to buy or sell. Tell the King he can keep his Gold Cow."

So 'Postle Jack led that cow back to the wagon and tied it up. Next he brought out the purple cloth and carried it back to the bank of Trouble Creek. He laid out that purple cloth on the ground, and he set to cutting it up, and sewing pieces of it together. 'Postle Jack spied them fellers eyeing him, and he called out cross the creek:

"This here's another one of them presents the King says I'm to give ye'."

"I'll bedad if'n I know what that is," that main feller shouts back.

"Why, this here's some of the King's Magic Cloth. If'n you make yourself a coat from this cloth, then anybody who wears it will be safe from robbers and thieves and what not."

"Well, there ain't no robbers and thieves what kin git into Corner Hollow," says the main feller, "seein' as how we built this wall and run off ever stranger what comes our way. So I reckon you kin jes' take that there purple cloth back to the King, with our thanks."

'Postle Jack gathered up that cloth and took it back to the wagon. He reached down his dulcimer and went back to the creek bank, where he commenced to playing.

"Now, this here's another one of them presents the King says I'm to give ye'," says 'Postle Jack as he strums the dulcimer louder.

"Why would we need one o' them from the King," says that main feller, "when we got a dozen of them already, with fellers who kin play better'n you."

"Well, this here's a enchanted dulcimer," says 'Postle Jack. "Whoever plays it will get his heart's desire brought to him."

"Humph," says the main feller. "I don't believe there's sech a thing. Besides, whatever our hearts desire is right here in our holler already. You go tell the King that he ain't got nothing we need." And with that, them fellers turned and left 'Postle Jack setting alone on the other side of the creek.

But 'Postle Jack just kept strumming on that dulcimer, and pretty soon, a whole passel of young'uns came wandering down to the wall, to see who was playing that music. Now, most of them young'uns climbed up on the backs of others, to see the stranger playing the dulcimer, then they'd shimmy on down and another one'd climb up and take a peek. But one little girl, with sweet summer-colored hair, she was so enchanted by 'Postle Jack and his music that she climbed right up to the top of that wall and stood up there just staring and smiling. If she'd been a bird, she might of just flown right up into the sky and circled his head with delight. 'Postle Jack kept strumming away, making music to enchant them young'uns , until all of a sudden-like, that little girl gave out a scream and fell right down to the ground and tumbled into the creek, where she lay, not moving nary a finger.

It weren't more than a moment afore that main feller came running out from behind the wall, just wailing and hollering. He scooped up the little girl in his big arms and stood at the edge of the creek, looking over at 'Postle Jack. "Do you have any magic that'll help my little girl, stranger?" asks the main feller.

"No sir, I surely don't have any magic like that," says 'Postle Jack. "But the King has some fellers over his way what can cure any thing what like to ail you. I know they'd be able to help your little girl. If'n you could carry her over to them, that is."

Well, that main feller, he set to barking orders to all them other fellers, and it like to took no time at all before they had that wall tore down and they were making a raft to carry that poor child over to the King's fellers. The main feller stayed right with his little girl all across Trouble Creek, and walked along the wagon as 'Postle Jack took them back to the King. It weren't but a day or two what that little girl was up, dancing and singing to 'Postle Jack's music, and that main feller thanked the King's fellers for what they had done for him and his child. When 'Postle Jack took that main feller and his little girl back to Corner Hollow, they had such a sight waiting for them. There weren't nary a trace of that wall, from side to side, anywhere in the mouth of that holler, and stretched across Trouble Creek was a wooden bridge, wide enough for a wagon, maybe even two.

Since that day, there were comings and goings from Corner Hollow to every other corner of the King's lands, until there weren't nobody what could say they hadn't walked across Trouble Creek Bridge. And everybody what's been there tells that Corner Hollow is right likely the prettiest spot in the whole of the King's lands, entire. The King was so pleased that he gave 'Postle Jack a wad of money, and that dulcimer what 'Postle Jack played for the children. And if you go to that corner of the King's lands, you'd be like to find 'Postle Jack setting somewhere's along Trouble Creek, at the mouth of Corner Hollow, strumming his dulcimer. Leastwise, last time I saw him, that's where he was.

'Postle Jack and the Invitation

———⫸◆⫷———

*The kingdom of heaven may be compared to a king who gave a
wedding banquet…. (They) went out into the streets and
gathered all whom they found, both good and bad;
so the wedding hall was filled with guests.*
Matthew 22:2, 10

———⫸◆⫷———

This here's the story of the time 'Postle Jack got involved with the King and his Revival. Now the King determined he would hold Revival. There would be preaching and singing and lots of food to eat. It would be the biggest, most powerful Revival there had ever been. So the King sent out invitations to the Revival. He invited all his friends from all over the county. Then he made his plans: he got him a preacher, set up a tent, hired him a choir of singers, and cooked him up a mess of food. But nobody came to the Revival. So the King went first to his nearby neighbor.

"Why ain't you at Revival, neighbor?" asks the King.

"Well, King, I just got too much to do to take time for Revival," says the neighbor. That made the King right mad, but he just went on his way, until he came to his cousin's house.

"Hey, cousin," says the King, "why ain't you at Revival?"

"Well, cousin," he says to the King, "I got to get my bean patch tended to. It needs to be picked something awful, and I hain't got nobody to help me. I cain't be taking time for no Revival. Not even your'n, cousin."

Well, the King was nigh on to taking a fit, but he didn't let on. He just headed on back to the tent and the Revival. But on his way, he ran into some other fellers he had invited to his Revival and he asked them why they didn't see fit to come.

"We don't like your dadburn Revival, King," these fellers say to him, "and we wouldn't be caught dead at it."

Well, you know the King was stomping mad now, and he was just about ready to tell them fellers what he thought of them, when 'Postle Jack walked by.

"Hello, King," says 'Postle Jack. "I hear you're having Revival."

"Law, Jack," the King says, "I got me a preacher fine as 'Postle Paul hisself. I got me a choir that can sing better'n a passel a' angels. I got me a big tent and all the fixin's for a big old feast."

"Why you look so put out, then, King?" asks 'Postle Jack.

"Cause, Jack, these fellers I invited are plumb full of excuses 'bout why they hain't a-coming. My neighbor's too busy, my own cousin is too busy, and the rest a' them fellers is jes' mean," says the King.

"Well, King, I can git you a crowd of folk at your Revival," says 'Postle Jack, "if'n you're willing to have 'em come."

"Jack, I'd be might pleased to have any comers," says the King. So the King went on up to the house, and 'Postle Jack, he went to find some folks for the King's Revival.

The first feller 'Postle Jack met was a old feller, used to work in the mines way back. He was old and tired now, setting on his porch, watching the world walk by.

"Hello, Father," says 'Postle Jack. "They's a Revival down at that big tent yonder. They's gonna be preaching and singing and a big old feast of food. King says you're invited. Will you come?"

"I'd be right pleased to come, 'Postle Jack," says the old man. "I'll be 'long directly, just soon as I clean up and get my go-to-meetin' clothes on."

"That's fine, Father," says 'Postle Jack, and he goes on his way.

The next feller 'Postle Jack met was a known scoundrel. Everybody knew he weren't nothing but a good-fer-nothing thief who never done a lick of honest work in all his days.

"Hello, Brother," says 'Postle Jack to the scoundrel. "They's a Revival down at that big tent yonder. They's gonna be preaching and singing and a big old feast of food. King says you're invited. Will you come?"

"Now, 'Postle Jack, you sure the King says I'm invited?" asks the scoundrel, looking suspicious at him. "Now, why would the King 'vite the likes a' me to his Revival?"

"Well, Brother," says 'Postle Jack, "I reckon if anybody is likely to need Revival, it'd be jes' folk the likes a' you."

"I reckon you's right 'bout that, 'Postle Jack," says the scoundrel.

"Will you come?" asks 'Postle Jack again.

"Well, I may be a thief and a scoundrel," says the scoundrel, "but I hain't gonna show no disrespect for the Lord. I'll be along directly, just as soon as ever I can rustle me up a clean shirt."

"That's fine, Brother," says 'Postle Jack, and he goes on his way.

Just then, 'Postle Jack run into a woman walking down the road with her three children.

"Hello, Mother," says 'Postle Jack. "They's a Revival down at that big tent yonder. They's gonna be preaching and singing and a big old feast of food. King says you're invited. Will you come?"

"Oh, law, 'Postle Jack," says the woman, "I surely would dee-light to come to Revival, but I got these three young'uns to look after."

"Why, bring them young'uns with you," says 'Postle Jack.

"Are ye sure that they'd be welcome, 'Postle Jack?" the woman asks. "They hain't never been to Revival, and they might holler and wiggle and not set still, like they should."

"Why, who ever hear tell of a Revival without young'uns squawking and squirming?" says 'Postle Jack. "It's jes' 'bout expected that they's there running underfoot. You bring them 'long, now, Mother."

"Why, thank you, 'Postle Jack," says the woman. "We'll be 'long directly, just as soon as I get their faces scrubbed good and clean for church."

"That's fine, Mother," says 'Postle Jack, and he goes on his way.

Well, 'Postle Jack did the same for everyone he met, good and bad, until that Revival tent was plumb full of folks. Some was setting, listening to the Preacher. Some was helping theirselves to plates of food. Some was crying, waiting for the choir to sing again. Some was old and feeble and some was young and noisy. 'Postle Jack just set back in the back and watched all them folks getting entertained and fed and spiritually satisfied. Just then the King showed up. Everybody allowed as how this was the finest Revival they'd yet been to in all their days. Each of them thanked the King for inviting them. Well, the King was right pleased with hisself and his Revival, and he knew he had 'Postle Jack to thank for it. So the King searched out 'Postle Jack to tell him just so. But setting there right next to 'Postle Jack was a ragged feller, who weren't nowise prepared to be at Revival.

The King says to 'Postle Jack, "Who is this here feller, Jack?"

"I don't rightly know, King. Just some feller who I happened by and invited him here."

"Look here, feller," says the King to the ragged feller, "why hain't you cleaned up and looking like you are coming to Revival?"

The ragged feller just looked at 'Postle Jack, and didn't say nary a word.

"Now, Brother," says 'Postle Jack, "didn't you know that this was Revival you was invited to?"

"Well, yes, Jack, I did, but…"

"And hain't you never knowed to do your best by yourse'f for Revival?" says 'Postle Jack.

"Well, yes, I knowed it, Jack, but…"

"All these other folk, they saw fit to get theirselves scrubbed clean and put on their go-to-meetin' clothes," says 'Postle Jack to the ragged feller. "How come you didn't see fit to present yourse'f best for the Lord?"

"Well, Jack, I was a'goin' somewhere's else when I ran into you and you invited me here. Seein' as how it was you that invited me, and seein' as how it was the King who was holding Revival and all, I felt obliged to a'tend. So I jes' came on in."

"Well, you jes' git on out, then," says the King to this ragged feller. "And don't you not come on back, neither."

Just 'bout that time, the choir set to singing, "Just As I Am, Without One Plea." All them others, the old miner, the thief, the mother, and the rest, they joined right in, singing just as loud as you please. But the ragged feller, he turned and went on his way. 'Postle Jack helped hisself to a big plate of food and commenced to eat his fill. The King went to sit next to the Preacher and several sinners got theirselves saved that day. And 'Postle Jack, he went on his way toward home, cause last time I saw him, that's where he was, and he was still wearing his go-to-meetin' clothes.

'Postle Jack Haints a Town

—————➤●◄—————

Wanting to justify himself, the lawyer asked Jesus, 'And who is
my neighbor?' Jesus replied, 'A man was going down from
Jerusalem to Jericho, and fell into the hands of robbers,
who stripped him, beat him, and went away'....
Luke 10: 29-30

—————➤●◄—————

Did you ever hear tell of the time 'Postle Jack got mistook for a haint? It weren't nowise his fault; it just happened to him kind of accidental like. It seems this young feller was leaving out of town to go make his way in the wide world. He had with him all his worldly possessions, which weren't even enough to shake a stick at, but it was all he had to his name. Well, no sooner had he started down the road when three robber fellers set on him, and beat him near to a pulp, took all his possessions, and left that young feller for dead in the ditch alongside of the road. That boy just lay there, barely stirring the grass with his breath, and praying that some good soul would come along and help him.

It just so happened that the local Preacher came along the road right about that time. He'd been off to Corner Hollow, preaching revival for the good folk there, and he was hurrying back to town to preach a week of revival at his own church. Now that Preacher Man saw that young feller laying in the ditch all beat up like that, and he figgered that boy was already dead. Seeing as how he was late for his revival, he just opened his Bible and pretended to read the Good Book, while he hurried on past what he imagined was that poor dead soul. Now to be fair, that Preacher Man sent a prayer winging its way off to heaven's ears for that boy's eternal soul, but he didn't stop or even slow down.

Well, a short while later, the Grocer came riding down the road in his wagon. He'd been off to the city, collecting all them vittles and such to sell at his store in town. The next day was market day, and he was figgering how much he needed to sell everything in his wagon for, so's he could make him back the money he'd done already spent, and a fair piece more to boot. When he saw that young feller just laying there in that ditch, all bruised and broken looking, he almost thought to stop and see what he could do for him. But then he began thinking, seeing as how the feller was probably already dead, and he had all them groceries and such, he just needed to get along back to the store. He thought maybe he'd send someone out to check on the feller, but he never did.

After a while, 'Postle Jack came walking down the road. Now as soon as ever 'Postle Jack saw that poor feller on the side of the road, he walked right over to him to see if'n anything be done to help him. When 'Postle Jack discovered how the feller had been beat near dead, but was still just barely alive, he scooped that feller up in his arms and carried him down the road toward town. It weren't long before 'Postle Jack spied a small cottage set back from the road, just out on the edge of town. 'Postle Jack, he just walked right up with that poor feller in his arms and commenced to hollering.

"Hello, house. Anybody to home?" hollers 'Postle Jack.

An old woman soon came to the door and opened it just a bit, so's she could spy out who was hollering on her front porch. When 'Postle Jack noticed how the door was open, he spoke right out to her. "Mother," he says, "this here poor boy is done beat near to death. Would you be so kind as to let me rest him here a while's, so's he kin git his strength back?"

"I'm just a poor widder woman," says the old woman, "but as long as I got a home, any stranger in need is welcome here."

"Thank ye, Mother," says 'Postle Jack, and he carried the young feller into the house and laid him on a cot in the corner of the kitchen. They took off the feller's tattered and torn clothing and cleaned his wounds. Since them robbers had done took all the feller's possessions, 'Postle Jack took off his own clothes and dressed the feller in them. Then, seeing as how he needed some clothes, 'Postle Jack dressed hisself in the tattered clothes of the young feller.

"Now, Mother, you give him ever what he needs, while's he's recuperatin', and I'll be back directly." And 'Postle Jack headed off into town.

It weren't long before 'Postle Jack came to the store owned by that feller what had just come down the road earlier in the day. 'Postle Jack walked hisself in there to see what supplies he might could get for the poor Widder Woman and that poor beat-up young feller.

"Hello, neighbor," says 'Postle Jack to the Grocer.

The Grocer looked at 'Postle Jack and blinked once or twice. "Don't I know you? Whose boy are ye?" says the man to 'Postle Jack.

"No, sir, I don't b'lieve as how you know me," says 'Postle Jack. "I'm not from around here. My people live a ways away, and I ain't never been here to your town afore."

"Well," says the Grocer, "I know I see'd you somewheres."

"Neighbor," says 'Postle Jack to the Grocer, "kin you give me some soup beans and some corn meal, and maybe a pound of butter and some eggs? I ain't got no money to pay for the food right now, but I'll pay ye before the day is out. If you kin, jes' send them groceries out to the home of the Widder Woman at the edge of town. She's took in a poor young feller what got beat by robbers and left for dead on the side of the road."

Just then, the Grocer recognized the clothes 'Postle Jack was wearing as the clothes he had seen on that feller in the ditch. His face flushed red, and he felt downright ashamed of hisself. "Listen, stranger," he says to 'Postle Jack, "I don't care a bit to take them groceries right out to the Widder Woman's house myself, and you don't owe me nary a cent for 'em, neither. If'n there's anything else what I kin do for ye, you jes' speak right up."

"Well," says 'Postle Jack, "lemme have one o' them penny whistles outta that bin there."

"Sure, help yourself," says the Grocer. And he hurried off to gather together soup beans, corn meal, butter, eggs, and a side of bacon for good measure.

Well, 'Postle Jack took a penny whistle and went on his way. It weren't long before he stumbled upon the Preacher Man setting to preach under a big tent in the middle of the town square. That Preacher Man was hopping and shouting and waving his floppy Bible this way and that in the air. 'Postle Jack stopped to listen, just for a moment. The Preacher was saying, "Now, fellers, when the day o' judgment comes upon you, our Lord is gonna want a reckoning of your deeds and your days. He's gonna wanna know if'n you done what he tol' you to do. Our Lord tol' us to love the Lord Your God with all your heart and all your mind and all your soul and all your strength. Now, if our Lord finds that you been holdin' back any of what you got in the way of your hard work from doin' the Lord's work, then he's gonna put you on his left hand with the goats and cast you into everlastin' fire."

About that time, the Preacher noticed 'Postle Jack standing at the edge of the tent, all dressed in the clothes of that poor feller on the side of the road. That Preacher, he took one look at what he figgered was the angel of that poor departed soul sent back to call him home, and he fell on his knees and commenced to hollering something awful. It took four deacons to lift that Preacher to his feet and get him calmed down enough to speak clear.

"Lord, I'm a worm and no man," says the Preacher at last, pointing at 'Postle Jack. "This here man is a angel come to convict me of my sin. The Lord says 'Love your neighbor as yourself,' and I left this man to die on the side of the road. Law, I'm ready for the eternal lake o' fire to consume me for my sin." And with that, that Preacher Man just fell over backwards and went right out on the ground.

The deacons looked at 'Postle Jack, afeared that he was a angel for sure, sent to take them all home. "I ain't that poor feller," says 'Postle Jack to the deacons. "But I know where he is. He's at the home of the Widder Woman at the edge of town, just as weak as he kin be."

Just then, that Preacher Man woke up, and when he heard what 'Postle Jack had told them others, he said, "Law, I got one more chance sure to please my Lord." And he told them deacons to take up a offering and carry that collection straight way to the home of the old Widder Woman.

Then he turned to 'Postle Jack. "Stranger, is there anything what I kin say to thank ye?"

"Well," says 'Postle Jack, "seein' as how it's gittin' 'long toward dark, I'd be right pleased to have one of them lanterns outta your tent."

"Take it, neighbor, and go in God's peace."

'Postle Jack left that tent and headed down the road, back out of town. He passed the spot on the road where that feller had been robbed, and he kept going a fair piece. It was dark and the moon was rising over the mountain when 'Postle Jack stopped and climbed up into a tree. He sat out on a branch over the road and waited. It weren't long before them three robbers came sneaking down the road back toward town. 'Postle Jack lit that lantern, hung it on the tree trunk next to his face. Then he commenced to blowing on that penny whistle. Them three robber fellers stopped dead in their tracks when they heard that whistle blowing in the tree tops. Then they spied the figure of a man what seemed to be floating up in the air above the road with what looked sure to be fire burning out of his head.

"Law, it's a haint," says the one robber to the others.

"It's that feller we done robbed today, for certain, come back to drag us to our graves," says another robber.

"Le's git shet o' this here cursed bag o' money, and p'raps that haint will spare us from the fires of hell," says the third robber. And them fellers dropped every last thing they was carrying, and went running off into the night, screaming and hollering, like they got the bejesus scairt out of them.

'Postle Jack clumb down out of that tree, and gathered up all what them fellers had dropped in their haste: them stolen possessions they took from that poor boy, a bag of money, and a shiny oak walking stick with a metal tip on one end and a strop of leather on the other. Then he took hisself back to the home of the old Widder Woman. When he got there, what he saw took him back.

"I'll bedad, if the whole town entire isn't at your house," 'Postle Jack says to the Widder Woman.

"Seems the Grocer and the Preacher Man went out and tol' ever'body 'bout this here poor feller, and me takin' him in," she says to 'Postle Jack. "They done carried in pies and cakes and jams, and ever' sort o' casserole you kin imagine. And the deacons say they is gonna fix up the porch on my house and put me up a load of wood for the winter."

'Postle Jack handed the bag of money to the Widder Woman and all them other possessions back to the young feller.

"Now, this here ain't my walkin' stick, Neighbor," says the young feller. "You take it, with my thanks."

So, 'Postle Jack, still dressed in the tattered rags of that poor feller, he took that walking stick, hung his lantern on the end of it, and headed out into the night, playing that penny whistle.

And some say, when the moon is full and the night is clear and the air is crisp and cold, you can see 'Postle Jack's lantern floating along the ridge of the mountains and you can hear his penny whistle playing in the tree tops.

'Postle Jack's Family Reunion

———⟶⟫●⟪⟵———

Ten bridesmaids took their lamps and went to meet the bridegroom. Five of them were foolish, and five were wise.
Matthew 25:1-2

———⟶⟫●⟪⟵———

Some of you might know that 'Postle Jack has two brothers, in addition to his mother and his father. Now his mother is a saint, and she's all the time trying to look out for her young'uns and 'Postle Jack loves her dearly. And his daddy, well, he's usually off to a job of work somewheres most days, and most nights when he gets home, he's right tired, but 'Postle Jack thinks the world of him too. But 'Postle Jack's brothers, Will and Tom, well, those boys are just as lazy as two good-fer-nothin' fellers can be, I reckon. And they are most all the time looking for how they can get by with doing nary a lick of work to help out around the homeplace. Seems like every time they's asked to do a chore, there's a reason it can't get done.

Now, it come to be the time of year for 'Postle Jack's family to hold Reunion just like they always do, and this year it was the responsibility of 'Postle Jack's parents to host the event entire, seeing as how Uncle Jake had hosted it the year before and it was getting along to be their turn anyhow. So they made all their plans and sent out a whole passel of letters to all their relatives, letting them know how it was time for Reunion, and what they should bring to the potluck, and when they should arrive and all. 'Postle Jack and his daddy set up the tent down by the creek and drug tables and chairs down from the church so's they would be places to set; Will and Tom were off hunting. 'Postle Jack's mother cooked up a mess of beans, and a apple stack cake, because those were her specialties and everybody always expected her to make beans and her famous apple stack cake. Pretty soon, all the family started showing up for the reunion and 'Postle Jack stood at the gate to greet everyone and direct them as to where to put all the food they carried to the reunion. Cousins were arriving from all over, and pretty soon, them tables was plumb full of shucky beans and boiled greens, pies and cakes of just about every variety there is, and a whole mess of chicken casseroles.

But Will and Tom weren't nowheres to be found; they was up the creek, fishing. 'Postle Jack went out looking for them, to invite them in to the Reunion, but when they seen him coming, they just laughed.

"Hey, brother," Will calls out to 'Postle Jack, "how's all them aunts and uncles of ours doing? Has any of 'em notice that you grow'd a little since last year?" This just makes Tom set to laughing harder than ever.

"They's all fine, brother," 'Postle Jack says. "They's all askin' after you two. Why don't you come down and set a spell with 'em."

"No thank ye', Jack," says Tom, trying not to laugh. "You go on back and tell 'em we'll be along directly."

"Directly after hit's over," Will adds, laughing hisself right down the bank and into the creek, where he splashes water all up into his boots.

"Now you done scairt off all the fish, Will," Tom hollers, and he set to cussing and fussing and causing a ruckus.

'Postle Jack just left them two boys carrying on there in the creek and went on back to his Family Reunion, where he set to standing at the gate again. By and by, a few neighbors came to the gate, carrying a pie and a fresh loaf of bread.

"Why, neighbor, what you doing here?" 'Postle Jack says to them.

"Well, we knew you was having Reunion here today, 'Postle Jack, and we figgered you could use a extra pie and a loaf a' bread to feed all your kinfolk. So, we jes' carried 'em on over, and here you are," says the neighbors offering the pie and bread.

"Why, that's right nice a' you, neighbors," says 'Postle Jack. "Why don't you'uns jes' come on in and join us at our Reunion?"

"Well, we ain't kin, 'Postle Jack," says the neighbors.

"Well, you're still welcome jes' the same," says 'Postle Jack, and he opens the gate and they walk right in.

A spell later, who should arrive at the gate but the King. Now, the King weren't nowise kin to 'Postle Jack, but still he lived nearby and he heard as how 'Postle Jack's family was having Reunion.

"Hello, King," says 'Postle Jack.

"Hey, 'Postle Jack, I see you'uns are having yourselves a Family Reunion."

"Yessir, King," says 'Postle Jack, "all my family is here, having theirselves a big ole time."

"Well, 'Postle Jack," says the King, "I'll tell you what I wanna do. You probably don't know it, but your daddy has allus' been good to help me ever when I needed the least thing. One time when I needed a fence mended, your daddy mended it for me, jes' quick as you please, and did a fine job of it too. Another time when I had a plot a' land that needed clearing, your daddy set to clearing it, and didn't stop til ever last stump was pulled up and burnt to charcoal. And once, when the Missus was feelin' poorly, your daddy brung over to the house a jar of beans and a apple stack cake your momma had cooked up fer us, jes' out a' kindness."

"I didn't know all that," says 'Postle Jack to the King, "but I ain't surprised, 'cause my daddy is a fine man."

"That he is, 'Postle Jack," says the King. "And I want to do somethin' to show how much I 'preciate him."

"King, my daddy don't 'spect you to show 'preciation to him for what he done," says 'Postle Jack.

"I know that," says the King, "but I wanna do it anyhows. I got with me here some a' the finest steaks I had cooked up, and a few gallons of my finest cider I had put up last winter. I want you'uns to have it fer your Reunion."

"Why, thank you, King," says 'Postle Jack. "That's right nice a' you. Why don't you come in yourself and celebrate with us?"

"I think I'll do jes' that," says the King, and he walks right through the gate.

At that very same moment, Will and Tom happened by. They were getting powerful hungry, seeing as how they had been out hunting and fishing and hollering in the creek all day, with nary a thing to show for it, except muddy shoes and wet britches. When the two of them saw the King walking through the gate, with a mess of fine cooked steaks and several gallons of the finest cider, they decided maybe it was time to go on in to reunion. So they ambled over to the gate where 'Postle Jack was standing and they stood looking at him, waiting for him to open the gate and let them in. But 'Postle Jack didn't open the gate.

"Open the gate, now, Jack," says Will, seeing all his cousins, and aunts and uncles setting to eat the King's steaks. "We's powerful hungry, and we need to get us something to eat."

"Go on, now, fellers. You go on about your business," says 'Postle Jack.

"Now, wait jes' a minute here," says Tom, looking at the neighbors lining up to eat the King's steaks too. "You done let them other fellers in, and they ain't even kin. We's your own kin, here, Jack, and you gonna turn us away?"

"You may be kin, but you ain't welcome," says 'Postle Jack. And with that he latched the gate and went on back to his reunion, where he got him a big old steak and a tall jar full of that cider and a big slice of his momma's apple stack cake, and 'Postle Jack set to celebrating with all his family. I hear tell that Reunion went on for a good long time, too. As a matter of fact, some say as how it might yet be continuing, and I don't doubt it, cause I know how 'Postle Jack loves a celebration.

'Postle Jack Plants Some Seeds

———⇒►●◄⇐———

Jesus told them many things in parables, saying:
'Listen! A sower went out to sow.'
Matthew 13:3

———⇒►●◄⇐———

Did you ever hear tell of the time 'Postle Jack planted some seeds? This weren't nothing like that time he picked beans, and he weren't really planting seeds. What he was doing was just being hisself. It happened like this.

'Postle Jack was walking down by the river bottom, where Upper Creek runs into Lower Creek to make Big Branch. It was that time of year when the water was low and the air was hot, and 'Postle Jack had a mind to dip his hat in the river to cool his head. So he slid on down the bank and leaned hisself over the water. Just about that time, he heard voices, and splashing and hollering, and when he looked up, there, in the middle of the river, were four young'uns, little tow-headed stairsteps.

"Hey there, children," 'Postle Jack started to say. But before he could even speak to them proper, the oldest boy tossed a big flat rock not two feet from 'Postle Jack. That rock hit the creek with a great whoop, and splashed water up into 'Postle Jack's face and soaked his shirt pretty near clean through. Them four children saw 'Postle Jack sputtering and dripping, and they all just fell out with laughing.

Now, 'Postle Jack weren't never one to stop a child from having his share of fun, but still, to get your shirt soaked when you weren't of a mind to have it soaked, well, it's like to set a feller to grumble. 'Postle Jack, he just looked at them young'uns , gave a quick smile to hisself, and hollered out with his meanest, most growed-up sounding voice.

"Whose young'uns are ye?" asks 'Postle Jack.

"We's the King's children," says the oldest boy. "Whatcha gonna do 'bout that?"

"I reckon I need to have me a talk with the King, then," says 'Postle Jack, and off he went, heading up the road. It weren't long before he spied the King's house. 'Postle Jack walked right up the path, onto the porch, and commenced to banging on the door. Right soon the King hisself came to the door.

"Why, hey there, 'Postle Jack," says the King. "What kin I do for ye?"

"Is that passel o' young'uns down yonder your'n, King?" asks 'Postle Jack.

"Why yes they are, as a matter of fact," says the King.

"Now, King, I ain't one to stop a child from having his share of fun," says 'Postle Jack, "but they like to soak me clean through, down at the creek jes' now."

"Law, 'Postle Jack, I do feel right bad 'bout that, you know, now. But kids will be kids."

"Why aren't they in school, learnin' all 'bout what they need to know 'bout life and sech?" asks 'Postle Jack.

"Well, you see, 'Postle Jack, there ain't any school nearby for them to be a-goin' to. I've done hired me some teachers up here to the house, but to tell you the truth, nary a one of 'em was worth a day's wages, when it came to learnin' my young'uns what they need to know 'bout life and sech."

"I jes' hate that for you, King," says 'Postle Jack. "Hit like to aggravate me no end to see young'uns growing up without the proper guidance and all, 'specially the King's children."

"Well, 'Postle Jack," says the King all of a sudden like, "I'd be right pleased to have you teach my children all you know 'bout life and sech. I'd hire you a fair day's pay for your troubles too, plus a bed and dinner each day to boot."

"I really ain't a teacher, King," says 'Postle Jack. "I'm more of a farmer, used to planting seeds and harvesting fields and the like."

"That's all teaching is," says the King. "You jes' plant what you know in them young 'uns, and it'll grow full up in no time, sure as certain."

"Then I'll jes' do that for ye, King," says 'Postle Jack, and they shook on it.

That evening, after a supper of soup beans and cornbread, 'Postle Jack set down his new pupils on the porch, and commenced to teaching them. Now he didn't teach them the regular book learning, stuff like figures and reading and such. Instead, he told them stories, all about life and such. He told them stories of all sorts, mostly about his adventures. He told them about the time he picked a entire hollow full of beans clean off the vine in only one day, and how two fellers tried to rob him, even after he paid them fairly. He told them about the time he went to Revival and sang loud as ever you please right alongside of mothers and young'uns and even no-account fellers, and how everyone else was too busy to join them in their singin'. He told them about the time his family held Reunion down by the river, and everybody came, bringing pots of shucky beans and fried apples, and how his momma made her famous apple stack cake, and how they even had juicy steaks and the finest cider, but his own brothers weren't nowise welcome into the feast, on account of their own meanness. And he told other stories too, about all the people he had met along his travels: old mothers who baked him up a loaf of bread, and young boys who looked scairt of their own shadows, and good fellers who just needed them a job of work to keep idle hands busy. And he told lots more stories, besides, more than you could set down in twenty books.

Now, 'Postle Jack didn't tell these stories all of a once, but every evening, just after supper and before the sun sank down over the mountains, 'Postle Jack would gather those young'uns on the porch and start to spin his tales. It weren't no easy task, captivating the attention of the King's children, even for a storyteller like 'Postle Jack.

The youngest of the King's sons, Little John, he was all the time worrying everybody to death with questions. When he heard tell of the Revival, he wanted to know why the King's friends and relatives couldn't come. "What were they doing?" he asked over and over again. "Why didn't they come?" And when he heard tell of the Family Reunion, he worried about all the people who were there, and what if they all brought soup beans and nobody brought the fried apples, well, wouldn't they just have lots of soup beans to eat? And when he heard tell of them fellers who ran off with 'Postle Jack's bag of beans, he feared for three days that they would show up on the porch looking for their sack of money.

There was the King's oldest daughter too, Missy Jane. Now Missy Jane just couldn't set still long enough for 'Postle Jack to get past his first sentence. She would be braiding her hair, or smoothing the quilt that hung on the back of the rocker. Or she would jump up in the middle of a story and set to sweeping the porch. Or she'd ask just the silliest questions, like what kind of clothes them people wore to the Revival, or did anybody show up at the Reunion without carrying a bit of food to share, or how much exactly is a wad of money, and could you buy yourself one of them store dresses with it.

And that oldest one of the King's children, Big Jim, now he was just plain bad; there weren't no two ways about it. He was always pulling his sister's hair, or scrapping with his brother, or spitting at the dog. He would interrupt 'Postle Jack's stories with shouts and taunts. When he heard about 'Postle Jack picking all them beans, he said, "Humph, I bet you did no sech thing." When 'Postle Jack told about the robbers setting on him, Big Jim cheered them on. When he heard tell of the old mothers and young boys 'Postle Jack met along his journeys, Big Jim called them names, just for spite. And one day, when it came of an evening, and hit was time for the children to be gathering on the porch, Big Jim was chasing the cat with a stick, the end of it burning red-hot as coal. When 'Postle Jack reached over to take that stick from him, Big Jim shoved it right into the palm of 'Postle Jack's hand. The other children watched and waited for 'Postle Jack to stomp and cuss and fuss, and slap him knock-kneed. Big Jim's mouth fell open and he just stood still too. But 'Postle Jack didn't stomp and holler; just one tear fell down his cheek, as he turned to climb the stairs to the porch. That evening he didn't tell stories; he sang some songs and played his dulcimer until the sky was pitch dark and the stars commenced to shining over every mountaintop.

The youngest of the King's children, her name was Mary Alice. She was most of the time quiet as could be, but she seemed to dearly love to hear the stories 'Postle Jack told of an evening. She sat right at his feet, her sparkling grey eyes shining up at him like fireflies flitting on a summer night. When 'Postle Jack told how he tricked them two fellers into stealing a sack of beans, Mary Alice laughed, and it sounded like the water in the creek tumbling over the rocky creek bed. When 'Postle Jack told about the King showing up at the Family Reunion with all them steaks and fine cider, Mary Alice clapped and shouted "Hooray." When 'Postle Jack told about the young boy who left home looking for a job of work, because his family was hungry and didn't even have bread to eat, little Mary Alice's eyes filled with tears, and she prayed for that little boy's family for a whole week each night before she went to bed. And when her oldest brother, Big Jim, finally allowed as how he'd had enough of setting on the porch and hearing fairy tales about children and old folks, and he swore he was setting out to find his own way in the world, Mary Alice gave him her very own handkerchief and wrapped a jar of rhubarb jam inside of it, and put it in his pocket.

One morning, after a long time of spending his days this way, telling his stories to the King's children, 'Postle Jack woke up to find frost on the ground and fog on the mountaintops. He went to the King and said as how he reckoned he had done told those children all there was for him to tell and how he ought to be getting along home, to help his own family get ready for the hard winter just around the bend.

"I thank ye, 'Postle Jack," says the King. "I reckon there hain't no better schoolin' my young'uns coulda had."

"Well, I don't rightly know 'bout that," says 'Postle Jack. "I cain't say as how I learned 'em an awful lot 'bout proper subjects. But they know as much 'bout life and sech as I do now, pret' near. And that's gotta count for something."

The King shook 'Postle Jack's hand and gave him a wad of money for traveling with. Big Jim was already long gone. Missy Jane was inside the house still trying to decide what dress to wear to send off a visiting storyteller. Little John was around back of the house, worrying about whether the ground would be too cold or too hard for someone to sleep on while traveling at night. Mary Alice stood next to the King and watched as 'Postle Jack put on his walking shirt and his old hat. Just before 'Postle Jack turned to go, she threw her arms around him and whispered, "I'll remember your stories forever and ever." 'Postle Jack patted her on the head and slung his dulcimer over his shoulder, and he set off on his way home.

Last I heard tell, the King's children were finding their own way in life. Big Jim wandered right far from home, and nobody hears tell of him much anymore. Missy Jane done went and got married five times in a row, but weren't none of them what you'd call "a good match." Little John spends his days counting the King's money and making sure that nobody cheats him out of what's his by rights. And Mary Alice, I hear tell, is a teacher. She has a whole passel of children in her classroom every day, and their favorite part of class is hearing all her stories about a feller named 'Postle Jack.

'Postle Jack Returns

———⟫●⟪———

Then Jesus said, 'There was a man who had two sons.'
Luke 15:11

———⟫●⟪———

Now most of you'uns know about 'Postle Jack, how he's always going about, traveling over the mountains and having all sorts of adventures in the far country. Well, this time, 'Postle Jack had been gone from home a good long spell, when he came walking up the hollow. His mother was out in the bean patch, weeding and planting, when she saw him from a long way off. She hollered off to 'Postle Jack's father to come on in from the corn rows and clean up for a big supper. Then she hurried off into the kitchen to cook up a mess of supper for her wandering son. By the time 'Postle Jack made it to the head of the hollow where the homeplace stood, he was right hungry, and he could smell his mama's soup beans simmering and cornbread baking.

It weren't long before 'Postle Jack, his mother, his father, and his two brothers, Will and Tom, were all setting down to a regular down-home feast of sorts. Course, there was soup beans and cornbread, certain. There was also a mess of greens, and turnips big as a fist, and tiny new potatoes dug fresh from the garden. In the middle of the table was a big platter laden down with thick slices of country ham. As the family ate their fill, 'Postle Jack told them all about the adventures he'd been having hisself off in the far country since he'd been away. And as he talked, and as they set listening, his brothers Will and Tom got madder and madder, until they was right worked up into a fit. That's when their mama fetched a delicious-looking apple stack cake from the kitchen and set it right in front of 'Postle Jack.

"Here, son," she says to 'Postle Jack. "I made this special for you, seein' as how it's your very favorite."

"Why, thank ye, Mother," says 'Postle Jack. "I feel right special now."

Well, seeing that their mama had made that special apple stack cake for their brother, Will and Tom finally jumped up and set to hollering and cussing and stomping their feet.

"How come you di'n't make us no special cake, Mother?" asks Will. "Me and Tom here, we been workin' hard all day, and you ain't made no special cake fer us!"

"And I don't 'low as how our brother is any specialer than any other feller," says Tom. "He's off all the time, wanderin' a far piece, tellin' tales, and doin' lord knows what else with all kinds of strange folk. Then he comes a-marchin' on home, like he's King-o'-the-Mount'in, and thinkin' he's more deserving than us'ns what's been here all 'long."

"Now, brothers," says 'Postle Jack to them, "I don't say I'm any specialer than nobody else. But this here is a celebration of sorts, and you'uns need to come on to it with us."

"How you mean that, brother?" asks Will, setting down again and staring at his younger brother.

"Well, lemme see. Did I ever yet tell you'uns 'bout the King's Midsummer Celebration?"

"No, sure as certain, we ain't heard word one 'bout no Midsummer Celebration, brother," says Tom, setting back down in his chair and leaning against the wall.

"Hit jes' so happened that ever year at Midsummer Night, I'd find myself right smack at the King's doorstep. And ever year, the same thing passed.

'Law, it's 'Postle Jack,' the King says to me. 'You ain't been through here in nigh on a year.'

'I guess that's jes' 'bout the way I figger it too, King,' I says back to him.

'You come on in, now, 'Postle Jack, and you be my guest at my Midsummer Celebration. You kin tell us some of your stories 'bout your adventures you been off havin'.'

'I reckon I ken stop and stay a spell,' I says to the King, 'and I'll be right pleased to tell some of my stories, if'n you think any of 'em is worth hearin'.'

"So I go in to the King's house, and that night he has him a feast fit for a King, sure 'nuff. They's whole pigs, cooked over a fire. And four different kinds of beans. And yellow squash and green squash, and other striped squash jes' drippin' with brown sugar and butter. And they's potatoes and red-eye gravy. And after supper they's fresh coffee brewed up dark, with sugar, and plate after plate of strawberry rhubarb pie, enough to make a body plumb sick with eatin'."

Will and Tom's eyes grew big as 'Postle Jack told them what all the King had laid out at his Midsummer Celebration, and their mouths set to watering and their stomachs set to grumbling. "Truth to tell, brother," says Will, "did ye really et all them things at the King's Midsummer Celebration."

"I bedad, Will," says 'Postle Jack. "They's all that and more, some what I cain't even recollect the names o' all them vittles."

"I swann," whispers Tom, leanin' forward a little to hear what 'Postle Jack would tell next.

"Now, ever year," 'Postle Jack says to his brothers, "ever year, jes' as supper is fixin' to be served, the King's son, Little John, not the other one, he come in and set down at the very end o' the table, jes' 'bout as far away as he kin git, yet still be in the same room as all that food, so's he kin still eat his fill, and he kin still hear the stories and the singin' an' all, but so's he kin act like he's right put out, not enjoyin' hisself at all. Ever'body could tell just from his face that he was disapprovin' of what his daddy the King was doin.'"

"Why, it ain't his place to be disapprovin' o' what the King does with his own fixin's," shouts out Tom, getting caught up in what he's hearing.

"Well, that may be, brother," says 'Postle Jack, "but that's the way he set his face, sure as I'm settin' here tellin' you 'bout it. So, the King, he gits up outta his chair, and he goes to the end o' the table, and he sets hisself down right next to Little John.

'Son,' the King says to him, 'son, why is it you come in here to my Midsummer Celebration ever year, and you set almost with your feet out the door and a scowl acrost your face, like you just bit into a wormy old apple?'

'I'm glad you as't me, King,' says Little John to his daddy, ' 'cause I been waitin' to tell you. Ever year, I work and work to keep your lands and watch over all that's your'n, so's it will bring you all what's good, and all what you got comin' to you. I work and work and work,' says Little John, his voice gittin' louder 'n' louder, til jes' 'bout ever'body kin hear what he is saying. 'I work ever dadblame day o' the year, 'n never onc't did you have no feast for me. But ever time this wanderin' storyteller shows up, you stop ever what you're doin' and fix up a feast like nobody's bidness, and invite all your kith and kin, pret' near the entire kingdom, to come eat your food and listen to his stories. Hit jes' don't seem right,' says Little John finally, looking down at his feet.

'I'll bedad, Son,' says the King to Little John, 'is that's what's got to ye? Little John, you are my son, and I love you more'n breathin'. Don't you know that ever what I got is your'n to do with as you please? But there is somethin' you don't yet know, son. The celebration is always here. The table is set ever' evenin', and the guests arrive ever' evenin', sure as certain, and the stories git told, and the songs git sung, and the feast is et, ever' night. It's jes', well, you are so busy keepin' track o' ever'thing, you jes' don't allus show up.'

"Law, li'l brother," says Will, "that King's son kep' hisself outta a mess o' good things, that's certain."

"If'n he'd a jes' fretted less and showed up more, he'd a been celebratin' ever' night," says Tom. "Turn's out he's the one what weren't 'lowin' hisself no joy, what with all that complainin' and throwin' a fit, an' all."

"Seems like he's so caught up that someone else might git somethin' o' what's his, that he's already missin' it," says their daddy, looking right at his two sons.

"Law, Jack," says his mama, "I got so caught up by your tale, I plumb clean forgot." She jumped up and hurried into the kitchen, and in no time at all, she come back with two whole pies. "This one is your'n, Will," she says. "It's strawberry pie, your favorite. And this here rhubarb pie is for you, Tom, entire, jes' like you like it, with sugar sprinkled 'cross the top of it." Will and Tom's eyes got big, looking at them two pies.

"How come you went and made us these pies, Mother?" asks Will.

"Yeah," says Tom, "we're jes' allus here."

"That's how come I made 'em, boys, 'cause you'uns is allus here. And that's worth celebratin' too."

With that, Will and Tom cut a piece of each pie, one for their mama, one for their daddy, and one for 'Postle Jack. Then they set to eating their pies entire theirselves.

"I sure am glad you come home, so's we kin celebrate," says Will to 'Postle Jack.

"I'm glad you come home, too, brother," 'Postle Jack says.

"I bet the king's table never did see no rhubarb pie like this one," says Tom, his face stained red, "not even at his Midsummer Celebration."

"No, brother, hit never did see the likes of it," says 'Postle Jack. And with a smile, he set to eating a great big slice of his special apple stack cake, and celebrating. For all I know, he's still there at home, celebrating with his kin. Leastwise, that's where he was last I seen him.

How 'Postle Jack Got His Call

———⫸●⫷———

And Jesus called them. Immediately they left the boat and their father, and followed him.
Matthew 4:21-22

———⫸●⫷———

This here's the story about how 'Postle Jack got his call. There's some what says 'Postle Jack's too hard for regular folk to take a liking to, seeing as how he's always doing whatever thing is the most true and right and good. But 'Postle Jack isn't really nothing more than just regular folk, like you and me, 'cepting he got his call, whereas some of us, well, we're still waiting to get ours. He finally got his call to be 'Postle Jack, but before he got his call, he was just folk.

Why, when Jack were a young feller, there were not one thing particular about him that would make you set up and take notice of him. Some days he was up early hunting him up a job of work, helping out his mother and his father, and being just as good as you please. Other days, he wouldn't do nary a lick of work, and he seemed about as good for nothin' as a boy can be. One day, as Jack was setting around with some other fellers, he heard them talking about the King.

"That King is mighty powerful," says one feller. "He might jus' be the mos' powerful man around, I reckon."

"And he's powerful rich, too," says another feller. "I hear tell he has sacks of money, jus' settin' around."

"Just 'bout ever man from here to Kingdom Come does just exactly what the King tells him to do, if'n he knows what's good for him," says a third feller.

"Well," Jack says to these fellers, "sounds like I need to be workin' for this here King, then, if I want to get me some of that power and money." So, Jack, he up and went to the King and asked him for a job of work.

"I'd be right pleased to have you work for me, Jack," says the King. So Jack took up with the King and lived right high for some time, in the shadow of the King's wealth and power. But then one day, a singer came to the King's house to entertain all the King's folk. This singer sang about faraway lands and strange beasts, the like of which Jack had never heard tell of. Then the singer sang a song about the devil dancing in fire and darkness. The King shuddered and told that singer to stop right quick, if'n he knew what was good for him.

"What's the matter, King?" Jack asks. "You ain't afraid of this devil person, are you, King?"

"Yes, Jack, I am," the King says. "The devil is right powerful and can make men do all manner of terrible things."

"But I figgered you was the most powerful man around," says Jack to the King.

"I may be a powerful man, Jack," says the King, "but I hain't got nothin' on that devil."

"Well, I reckon I better be gittin' 'long, then, King," says Jack. "I aim to serve the most powerful one around, so I'll be lookin' for that devil."

"I hate to see you go, Jack," says the King. "You been a right good worker, and I been pleased to have you serve me." And as a parting gift for all his good work, the King give Jack a small sack of money, some bread for his journey, and a small wooden cross carved from the branch of a dogwood tree, and tied on a leather strap to hang around his neck. Jack thanked the King for his kindness and set off to find the devil.

It weren't no time at all before Jack happened upon a couple fellers that were hiding along the roadside, waiting to jump on anyone what passed by and steal whatever they might could take. These two fellers were right mean and ugly too. They jumped out as soon as Jack were within sight. "Hello there, traveler," says these two ugly fellers to Jack. "Give us all you got."

Now Jack saw as how these fellers meant business. So he pulled out his sack of money. "This here is money the King give me, fellers. I reckon you're welcome to it," says Jack, "but you sure will make the King mad, if'n you take his money."

"We don't care 'bout no King," says one feller. "Let the Devil take him," says the other.

"Strange you should mention the Devil," says Jack. "I'm lookin' for that Devil. Do you know where's I can find him?"

"We serve him," says the first feller. "And we'll take you and your sack of money to him."

So those fellers led Jack to a dark cave up a hollow, where the Devil was making his plans. But when that Old Devil seen Jack coming, why he screamed and stomped and commenced to hollering at him. "But, Devil, sir," says Jack, "I hear tell you are the most powerful one around, and I aim to serve you."

"If you aim to serve me, Jack, then you'll need to get shet of that wooden cross hanging there around your neck," says the Old Devil.

"Devil, why are you so aggravated by this here little wooden cross?" asks Jack.

"There once was a feller named Jesus Christ who was killed on a cross, but he beat even death itself, and now he lives forever, and all his followers too. I don't care a bit for them and their symbols of hope. That there cross is the symbol of his followers," says the Devil. "If'n you want to serve me, Jack, you get shet of it."

"Well, Devil," says Jack, "I aim to serve the most powerful one around and it seems to me like this Jesus Christ must be more powerful even than you. So I best be on my way." And with that, Jack took his leave of them mean ugly fellers, and didn't even look back.

Now all Jack had left was two loaves of bread the King had given him for his journey. After he had walked a far piece, he got hungry and sat hisself down and commenced to eating one of those loaves of bread. Just about that time an old woman came walking up the road and stopped in front of Jack.

"Traveler, I'm powerful tired and hungry," says the old woman to Jack.

"Well, mother," says Jack to the old woman, "you just set down here and I'll share my loaf of bread with you. It's not much, but it's all I got, and it will give you strength I know."

"Thank ye, kind sir," says the old woman, and she sat and ate her fill of bread from Jack's loaf. After a time, Jack got up and turned to the old woman. "I best be off now, Mother. I'm lookin' to find Jesus Christ. He's the most powerful one around, 'cause he done beat death, and all his followers done beat it too. I aim to serve this Christ, if'n he'll have me."

"Well, good luck to you, and thank ye for the meal," says the old woman. "I know you'll find who you're lookin' for." And she waved as Jack went on down the road and wandered out of sight.

It weren't too long before Jack saw a young boy sitting by the side of the road, crying.

"What's got you crying, brother?" says Jack to the boy.

"My daddy says we ain't got enough to feed all us young'uns what lives at home," says the boy to Jack. "So he says I have to go out on my own now, and make my way in the world, find me a job of work or go to the devil, one."

"Well, brother," says Jack, "I tell you what you do. You take this here loaf of bread home to your daddy and all them other young'uns. Then you go on over to the King's house and you ask him to give you a job of work. Tell him Jack sent you."

"What if the King don't believe me, Jack," says the boy, wiping his nose on his sleeve and looking hungrily at that loaf of bread.

Jack took the little wooden cross off hisself and hung it around the boy's neck. "Show this here cross to the King, and tell him Jack give it to you," says Jack. "This here is the sign of the most powerful one around, a feller by the name a' Jesus Christ, who I aim to serve. Now git on home, brother."

"Thank ye', Jack," says the boy, and he skipped away with the cross around his neck and the loaf of bread under his arm.

Jack started on up the road, but as soon as he made the next turn in the road, right there in the middle of the road was a dogwood tree. It grew straight and tall as a man, with only three branches; one to the left, one to the right, like arms, and one straight up. Jack stared at it and says right out loud, "Why, tree, what are you doing right here in the middle of the road?"

To his sudden surprise that tree answered right back to him. "I'm the one you seek, Jack."

"I'm seeking Jesus Christ, the most powerful one in all the world, the one who beat death and is the King of Life," says Jack. "I aim to serve him."

The dogwood tree began to move and seemed to grow arms and a face, until it looked like the old woman. "When you gave me bread, you served me," says the face of the old woman. Then the tree shifted shape again and looked like the young boy. "When you helped me and my family, you served me," says the face of the boy. Then the three branches of the tree burst into bloom, until they were covered with little white blossoms. "Go and tell people about me, 'Postle Jack," says the tree, "and you will be serving the One you seek." Then the wind blew all the blossoms off the branches and they covered the ground at 'Postle Jack's feet, and the tree shrunk until it was the size of the little wooden cross that 'Postle Jack had given away. He picked up the cross and put it in his pocket and headed down the road.

And he's still traveling that road, telling people about the One he serves, doing what he can to help folk. Leastwise, that's what he was doing last time I saw him.

What 'Postle Jack Gave

———>»•«<———

For it is as if a man, going on a journey, summoned his slaves
and entrusted his property to them; to one he gave five talents,
to another two, to another one, to each according to his ability.
Then he went away.
Matthew 25:14-15

———>»•«<———

Did you ever hear tell of what 'Postle Jack gave to his homeplace when he set off on one of his adventures? It seems 'Postle Jack had been home for quite some time, and all his neighbors and kin were getting right used to having him around. So they came to him and asked him not to go off.

"Well, they's other places filled with other people what needs to hear my tales," says 'Postle Jack. "But I won't leave jes' yet. And 'fore I go, I'll give ye somethin' what'll make ye glad to have it." So, 'Postle Jack, he spent the next few days wandering around, visiting all those neighbors and kin what had said something to him.

One of his first stops was at the Weaver's home. She was a kind, gentle woman, who had a talent for weaving sturdy, warm cloth, and she had made the cloak what 'Postle Jack always traveled with.

"Now, Mother," says 'Postle Jack to the Weaver, as soon as he steps into her house, "you know that loom o' yor'n; that's a magic loom, it is. If'n you stand in front of it 'fore you go to sleep of an evening, and you say to it, 'Weave, loom, weave,' why, it'll set right to work weavin' the most beautiful cloth you ever did see, til by sunrise you'd have more bolts o' cloth than you could weave in a month."

"Law, Jack," says the Weaver, "who ever did hear tell of sech a thing? You jes' git on with ye, and don't pay us no mind, now. We'll be right fine, til you come on home." And the weaver give 'Postle Jack a scarf of fine warm wool, to keep the cold from his neck during his wanderings.

Later that day, 'Postle Jack stopped in to see his cousin, the Baker. Now everyone knew far and wide about that Baker and his biscuits and corn muffins, how they were the best anybody ever did eat. 'Postle Jack said as much while the Baker filled 'Postle Jack's satchel with enough corn muffins to last him a week of walking.

"Cousin," says 'Postle Jack, pointing over to a cracked old wooden bowl, "that there bowl a settin' on that shelf is a magic bowl. All's you'd have to do is reach it down, set it on the table at night 'fore you lay your head down on your pillow, say to it real stern-like, 'Fill, bowl, fill,' and when you'd git up of a mornin', your table'd be covered with fresh-baked breads and rolls, and no tellin' what all."

"I bedad, Jack," says the Baker, "I never did hear sech foolishness. Ain't you got yourse'f enough o' them muffins without you goin' and tryin' to butter me up for more. Git on with ye, and tell them tales somewhere's else." So, 'Postle Jack left the Baker's shop.

It weren't long before 'Postle Jack came to a quiet little house, way up at the head of the hollow. This was where the Old Craftsman lived. Most everybody knew him, but they almost always stayed away, on account of he was mean and ornery. Time was he made the most beautiful pieces of furniture from poplar and pine and cherry, trees he cut hisself from off the mountainside. They was so pretty, even the King had sent word to order hisself a new throne made by the Old Craftsman once. But them days was long gone, and now the old man just kept to hisself mostly.

"Neighbor, you inside here? " 'Postle Jack calls out, as he stumbles onto the porch. "I come to git me a sturdy new walkin' stick for my journey."

"Well, come on in, if ye must," says the Old Craftsman.

"Why, Neighbor, look at that there fiddle, jes' hangin' on your wall like that. That's pret' near the best lookin' fiddle I done seen."

"I made that there fiddle, 'bout 40 year' ago, for my boy," says the Old Craftsman, "but he never did live to learn it, and now I keep it there for *in memoriam.*"

"I di'n't know you could make magic fiddles like that," says 'Postle Jack. "That there is a magic fiddle. If'n you take it down from the wall and set it on the rocker, and tell it, 'Play, fiddle, play,' why it'll set to playin' a jig what'll make your heart dance."

"I swann, Jack," says the Old Craftsman, "there ain't no sech fiddle, and if'n there were, that th'ar fiddle ain't one o' them. Now, take your walkin' stick and be off with ye', 'fore I whop your backside with it." So 'Postle Jack left the Old Craftsman's house and headed up over the mountain and on his journey.

It weren't but a week before winter set in with a cold wind blowing up and down that hollow. The townspeople came running to the Weaver, asking her if she could make them some new warm clothes to keep out the bitter cold. But after only a day, she was plumb out of cloth, and had nary the strength to stay up all night weaving more.

Then, of a sudden, she remembered what 'Postle Jack had said about her loom being a magic loom and all.

"Well, I don't put no truck in sech nonsense," she says to herself right out loud, "but if 'Postle Jack says it..." She took a deep breath and stared straight at that loom, and said, "Weave, loom, weave." Then she turned out the light and went straight to bed. The next morning, she woke just before sunrise to find her floor covered with the prettiest cloth she ever did see, bolts and bolts of it. And it was sturdy and warm to boot. By dinnertime she had new clothes cut for every child in the town. That night, she stood again in front of her loom and spoke the words, "Weave, loom, weave." And again, she woke to a floor covered with new-made bolts of cloth. It weren't long before everybody in town had a new set of clothes cut from that cloth. The Weaver collected the scraps from her cloth, sewed them into beautiful patchwork quilts and sold them far and wide. She became known across the King's land for her perfectly woven cloth and her lively warm quilts, and she was blessed with good fortune.

Now everybody was right warm with their new clothes, but winter dragged on for months and lasted into the planting season. Nobody could plant their gardens on account of the frost that held the ground solid, and soon neighbors' supplies of shucky beans and pole beans and potatoes they had put up for the winter started to run low. The Baker did his best to cook up enough biscuits and corn muffins and breads and such, so nobody would go hungry. But soon, even he ran out of flour and corn meal and lard. He looked at his bare cupboard and began to sigh. Just then, he remembered about what 'Postle Jack had told him about that old cracked wooden bowl. So he reached it down, set it on the table, and said to it, just like it were a wayward child, "Fill, bowl, fill." Then he went off to bed, his belly just growling.

When he woke up of a morning the Baker found his table laden down with all sorts of breads and pastries and biscuits and muffins, some he didn't even know the name to call them. Soon, the smell of fresh-baked goods brought neighbors running to his shop, and he sold them loaves of bread and biscuits by the dozen until there weren't but scraps left. That night, just before he took hisself off to bed, the Baker looked at the old bowl again, and says, "Old friend, fill, bowl, fill."

Sure enough, come morning his table was covered again with all sorts of good things to eat. Soon, that bakery became known across the King's land for its savory goods; even the King sent word for the Baker to send along several cakes and pastries each week, in return for a big sack of money, and the Baker was blessed with good fortune.

But winter lingered, and time for summer came and went, with no sign of the warm days it always brings. The people of the town had new clothes to keep them warm against the cold, and they had all the warm bread they could care for, to stave off hunger during the long dark days. But still they seemed to malinger, until their eyes seemed as dark as the winter nights. The old folks, why they just shut theirselves up in their rooms, blanketed with quilts, and talked of the old days, back when they used to dance of a summer's evening. The young'uns , they didn't have sech membrances to keep to theirselves, and, one by one, they took theirselves off from that town, in search of summer and a place where they could dance in the sun, until there weren't but the smallest of children left, them what was too small to wander away, and them what was already too old to get shet of that town. And winter seemed to settle in for good up at the head of that holler.

About that time 'Postle Jack happened to come home. He took one look at his hometown and threw up his hands to the sky.

"Law, Neighbor, what in tarnation has took hol't o' this town?" asks 'Postle Jack, jes as soon as he finds someone what ain't hiding indoors.

"Winter ain't never left us, 'Postle Jack," says the neighbor, "and we cain't git shet of this here darkness nohow. The Sun has done gone and hid from our holler."

'Postle Jack up and went right to the home of the Weaver, and asked her, di'n't she use the loom like he said. "Sure, Jack, jes' like you tol' me, it weaved the prettiest bolts of sturdy, warm cloth. Cain't you see that ever'body in town has a new outfit what's made from that cloth!"

"Then why are their hearts as cold as the winter wind?" says 'Postle Jack.

"I wish I could say," says the Weaver.

Next, 'Postle Jack hurried over to the Baker's shop, and asked him if'n he used the magic bowl like he tol' him. "Jes' like, Jack. I set that bowl down on the table, tol' it ever' night, 'Fill, bowl, fill,' and ever' mornin' my table was full to bustin' with cakes and breads and I cain't say what all. Not one person what as't went without somethin' warm to eat."

"Then why are their souls as empty as their cupboards?" says 'Postle Jack.

"That I cain't tell ye', Jack," says the Baker.

Finally, 'Postle Jack went to the home of the Old Craftsman at the head of the holler, and asked him if he had played that fiddle with them magic words he done tol' him.

"I ain't done no sech thing," says the Old Craftsman. "This here is no magic fiddle, and I don't b'lieve in sech foolishness. B'sides, I made this fiddle for my dear son, long passed, and if'n he cain't fiddle on it, cain't nobody fiddle on it."

'Postle Jack, he jes' reached down that fiddle from the wall of the old man's hut, and headed back into town with it. He was walking so fast past the home of the young Widder Woman, that he almost didn't hear her young'un gasp as he came by.

"Well, hey there, young'un," says 'Postle Jack.

"That's the most beautiful, most special fiddle I ever did see in all my life," says the little tow-headed boy. "It must be a magic fiddle, sure."

"Well, I'll bedad," says 'Postle Jack to the boy, "that's jes' what it is, certain. And if'n you take it in your hand, and lay the end on your shoulder, like this, and tell it, 'Play, fiddle, play,' why, that's jes' what it'll do."

The young boy took the fiddle from 'Postle Jack, gentle as a kitten, and put it on his shoulder, just so. Then, with the bow in his other hand, the boy looked up at 'Postle Jack, shut his eyes down tight, and shouted, "Play, fiddle, play."

Well, that fiddle set to playing a jig so lively that little young'un set to laughing. And the sound of his laughter mingled with the music of the fiddle as it echoed off the mountainsides and clear up to the head of the hollow, where it scairt away Old Man Winter, who went off to make his home in Outer Darkness.

'Postle Jack in Paradise

———⟫⟩●⟨⟪———

Is not life more than food, and the body more than clothing?
Look at the birds of the air:…
Are you not of more value than they?
But strive first for the kingdom of God and his righteousness,
and all these things will be given to you as well.
Matthew 6:25-26

———⟫⟩●⟨⟪———

Now you may have heard about 'Postle Jack's adventures in the hills and hollows of the Appalachian mountains, but did you ever hear tell of the time 'Postle Jack ventured to the great Rocky Mountains? Well, it happened like this. It seems 'Postle Jack was at the King's house of an evening, when a traveling storyteller arrived. This storyteller sat at the King's table and told everybody what was there all sorts of tales of lands far and wide. He told of oceans of water that washed against the shores, kissing the land with every wave. He told of fields of grain and corn and beans that went on as far as the eye could see, waving like the ocean. He also told of mountains high and majestic, higher than anybody could imagine, towering so high up into the sky, they seemed to brush right up against heaven itself.

"Now, I never did hear tell of such mountains before," says 'Postle Jack to that storyteller. "I surely would like to see them towering mountains myself."

"Well, that's what you should do, then, certain," says the storyteller to 'Postle Jack. "There's places out there what are so beautiful they'll catch your breath right away from you. Hit's a land of promise and opportunity, for them what has a mind to see it as sech."

Right then 'Postle Jack made up his mind to find that land of promise with the towering mountains and breathtaking valleys. So, next day 'Postle Jack loaded hisself down with two loaves of bread, three jars of rhubarb jam, a handful of jerky, his jelly-jar lantern, his walking stick, and his dulcimer. Then he set out walking west. Well, I don't have to tell you, it took a mighty long time for 'Postle Jack to reach them mountains, and he had other adventures along the way, but they are part of other stories. Suffice it to say that 'Postle Jack finally came in sight of them towering mountains, and it was just like the storyteller had said: majestic purple mountains reaching up to touch heaven, and stretching up and down the land for as far as the eye could see. 'Postle Jack just stood and stared at that sight for a good long time, before he headed into the nearest valley at the foot of the closest mountains.

Well, it weren't long before 'Postle Jack happened upon a sign along the edge of the road. "Paradise, Colorado," it said, "Elevation: 7,143 feet." 'Postle Jack stood staring at that sign, until an old man came walking by.

"Hey, stranger," says the old man to 'Postle Jack, "what brings you to Paradise?"

"Well, grandfather," says 'Postle Jack, "I heard tell of a land of promise and opportunity away west in the towering mountains, so I come to find it."

"Then you'd best keep walking," says the old man. "This ain't that place. There ain't nothing here but dying dreams and forgotten people, most even older'n me."

'Postle Jack looked around, at the green valley nestled against the feet of two grand mountains, the sparkling stream running through the town and past the road, the patches of wildflowers that covered the banks and the valley floor, and the cozy town built up right in the middle of it all. "This sure looks like the right place to me," says 'Postle Jack. "Why ain't you more of a mind to see it, grandfather?"

"If'n you want to hear tell what happened to this town," says the old man, "I'd be right pleased to tell you, but you'll need to come set a spell with me."

"That I'll do, and be right pleased," says 'Postle Jack, following the old man into the middle of the little village, and up the front steps of what said it was Paradise Town Hall. The old man opened a door what had the word "Mayor" painted in big black letters on it, and pointed 'Postle Jack to a chair near the window. 'Postle Jack set down and stared out the window, wondering what could have happened to make such a land of promise into a land of sadness, like the Mayor had said.

"See that tipple up at the head of this valley?" says the Mayor of Paradise to 'Postle Jack.

"Yessir, I surely do," says 'Postle Jack. "Where I come from, the hills and hollers is dotted with tipples jes' like that one, to bring out the coal from deep in the earth."

"Just so," says the Mayor. "This here town was a mining town once't. About a hundred years ago, a wandering speculator with no more than a dream and a shovel found something worth settling down for right here. But it weren't coal. It was silver, and there was a right good bit of it in these mountains around this valley. A sharp mining town grew up quick and flourished here for a time. But then, all the silver got mined out, and all the promise and opportunity what came with it, left with the last bit of it too. That was more'n fifty years ago. We've just been growing older, since, watching all our children move off to the city, and watching all our businesses close down, and watching all our neighbors get buried. Now, there ain't nothing left of Paradise, excepting a few old folks, them what is too tired to leave town, and a few children, them what hasn't growed up enough yet to leave."

'Postle Jack just set quiet, staring out the window, thinking on what all the Mayor had said. He watched a woman with a clump of children around her walking through the village and up the road toward the mountains. They were carrying something with them he couldn't quite make out. Then, of a sudden, 'Postle Jack jumped up out of his chair. "Mr. Mayor, sir, thank ye for your time," says 'Postle Jack. "Do you mind if I wander for a spell here in your valley?"

"I'd be right pleased to have you here in Paradise for as long as you care to stay," says the Mayor to 'Postle Jack.

So 'Postle Jack thanked the mayor and went on his way, hurrying after that clump of children he had seen from the Mayor's window. As soon as ever he caught up with them, he could hear them laughing and singing as they walked along beside the stream.

"Mother, where are you'uns goin'?" says 'Postle Jack to the woman what seemed to be leading all the children.

"We're off to collect wildflower honey," says the woman.

"The bees make it way up at the head of the valley," says a little boy with eyes as blue as the big sky above the mountains.

"Do ye mind if I tag along?" asks 'Postle Jack.

"Not at all," says the woman who first spoke. "We'd be glad to have your company." So 'Postle Jack followed them up the stream, through the valley, right to the foot of that old tipple, and there he saw an amazing sight. Nestled in the rotting beams and boards of that contraption were about a hundred beehives, and about a million bees were swarming all around, flying out toward the wildflowers in the valley, and flying back, bringing with them what they needed to fill their hives with honey. The little blue-eyed boy walked right over to the nearest hive and waved his hand, laughing. The bees just seemed to fly right away, and he reached inside and pulled out a comb dripping with honey. He plopped it right inside a jar he was holding and started to move on to the next hive. 'Postle Jack watched as all the children took jars out of their sacks and began collecting honey just the same way from all those hives, until their jars were just about filled.

"Here, you can gather some too," says a little girl with hair the color of daisies, and she led 'Postle Jack over to a hive too high for her to reach. "Just wave at the bees and say hello, then they'll let you have some of their honey." 'Postle Jack did just as the little girl said, waving his hand hello at the bees, then he reached into the hive and pulled out the biggest honeycomb he had yet seen. It was so big he had to break it in half and put each half in a separate jar. He started to hand the jars to the little girl, but she just looked at him, saying, "Those are yours to keep." Then she danced over to join her friends.

'Postle Jack licked the honey off his fingers, and his face lit up, for this was the sweetest, most delicious thing he had yet tasted, better even than his precious rhubarb jam he had brung from back home, maybe. The children had filled all their jars and the woman was gathering them up to walk back toward the village. They were all singing and laughing in the late afternoon sun. 'Postle Jack fell silent, looking around this magical place. Then, of a sudden, an idea sprang to his mind and he hurried back to town.

'Postle Jack came strolling into town just as the sun was going down behind the mountains. It was getting to be about church time, as it was Sunday evening, and the citizens of Paradise were making their way to the big church meetinghouse in the center of town next to the town hall. 'Postle Jack walked right up the steps of the church and set hisself down in the front pew. All the citizens of Paradise poured into the church, wondering at this stranger what had seemed to appear out of nowhere, like the ghost of a mountain man from days long gone.

Now the Mayor was the one what led church services on Sunday evenings most times. So he stood up and welcomed all the citizens of Paradise to church with the usual greeting. Then he looked over at 'Postle Jack and began speaking.

"Neighbors," says the Mayor to all the gathered citizens of Paradise, "we have a special visitor with us today. He came in to town just this morning, full of wonder and questions. I did my best to tell him of our community." The Mayor looks over at 'Postle Jack again, and says to him, "Well, friend, if you have a mind to, bring us a word, would you?"

'Postle Jack stood up and looked out over the faces of the citizens of Paradise gathered in that place. Then he reached around his dulcimer what was slung across his back and began to play a light-hearted tune. All what heard that music began to think of sparkling streams and fields of wildflowers and wide open skies and breathtaking mountains, and their hearts were filled with joy and their spirits began to dance. Then 'Postle Jack began to speak.

"Way off back at home," says 'Postle Jack, "I heard tell of a place what was so beautiful it would take my breath from me. I heard tell of mountains so high their peaks brushed right up against heaven itself. I heard tell of a land of promise full of opportunity, for them what had a mind to see it as sech." Looking into the faces of the children and the old folks, 'Postle Jack says, "So I set out to find that land of promise I heard tell of, and my footsteps led me right here, to Paradise."

Just then, a man sitting way in the back of the church stood up and called out to 'Postle Jack. "Now listen here, stranger," says the man. "This here place ain't that place you heard tell of. This is no land of promise; this is just an old dying place. We ain't got no silver left in the mountains, and all our children move away off to the city to find their opportunity. There's nothing here what would make a mountain town thrive."

"But your mountain tops ain't shorn off," says 'Postle Jack to the man. "And your valleys aren't filled in and your spirits aren't broke."

"But our dreams are dead, and our hope is gone," says a tired-looking woman from another corner of the crowd. "Nobody wants to live in a mining town with nothing to mine."

"That's where you're wrong, mother," says 'Postle Jack to the woman. He reaches into his pack and pulls out those two jars full of golden liquid, and lifts them up for all to see. "This here is wildflower honey. Your valley is full of wildflowers, and them patches of wildflowers is full of bees. And them bees is busy making the sweetest honey I ever did put in my mouth. I followed your own young'uns today right to where there's enough honey to fill a whole passel of jars to overflowing."

"We know it's good honey," says the woman what had taken the children up into the valley. "We eat it all the time. But how is honey gonna help bring life and hope back to Paradise?"

"You tell people about the wonders of Paradise," says 'Postle Jack, "and I know this will be a land of promise and opportunity again." And with that, 'Postle Jack picked up his walking stick and strode right out the door of the church and headed out of town, back the way he came.

The citizens of Paradise were all buzzing with what they had heard. It weren't long before the Mayor called a meeting of the town leaders, and they began planning for a Wildflower Honey Festival. They sent notice to the towns all around that they were having a festival. Several people even made colorful posters, painted with wildflowers and bees, and sent them to relatives in the city to post there. The children collected more and more jars full of that sweet wildflower honey, and the old folks set to fixing up their village, until it fairly sparkled like the stream in the sunshine. On the day of the Wildflower Honey Festival, more than five thousand people came to Paradise to get those jars of honey, and to see the wildflowers, and to hike in the mountains, and to picnic by the stream. Some what came for the festival that day came back later. Some were artists who wanted to paint the beauty of the mountains and capture the colors of the wildflowers. Others were lovers of beauty, looking for a place that would fill their hearts and lift their spirits. Still others were the grown children what had moved off to the city and forgotten how Paradise always felt like home. Soon, Paradise was a thriving mountain village, a land of promise and opportunity. And the Wildflower Honey Festival was known far and wide as the highlight of every summer in Paradise.

'Postle Jack took those two jars of golden sweetness home with him, and he gave one to the King, and he left the other for the traveling storyteller who first told him about the land of promise.

'Postle Jack 'Tends a Wedding

—⟹➤●◄⟸—

On the third day there was a wedding in Cana of Galilee....
Jesus and his disciples had also been invited to the wedding.
John 2:1-2

—⟹➤●◄⟸—

This here's the story of the time 'Postle Jack 'tended a wedding. He weren't getting hitched hisself, mind you. He were just wandering past the King's house one day when he spied the King back to the side of the house, directing a passel of fellers setting up a big tent.

"Hey, King," calls 'Postle Jack. "What're ye up to, with this here tent and all these fellers?"

"Why, 'Postle Jack, ain't ye heard?" says the King. "My son, Little John, is fixin' to git married, and we're having ourselves a big ol' shindig day after tomorrow. We'd be right pleased if'n you'd see your way clear to join us."

"Law, King," says 'Postle Jack. "Little John gittin' hitched, huh? Well, I cain't miss somethin' as powerful as that now, kin I? I'll be there, King, the Good Lord willin' and the creek don't rise."

With that, 'Postle Jack waved to the King and headed off down the road, just about the time a big clap of thunder bust out over the mountains. Well, it rained for two days straight, and the King began to despair about all his preparations for the wedding. But, come the big day, the sun broke through the clouds late in the day, and shone just as big and bright as you please when it come time for the shindig.

All sorts of folk were gathered under the tent next to the King's house to see Little John and Kelly Jo get married. There was Little John's big sister, Missy Jane, and her husband of the moment (it was her third one). There was Mary Alice and some of the school children. Course, the King was there, and all his neighbors and kin. Them folks were setting to talking and socializing, waiting for the festivities to start, when 'Postle Jack arrived with a passel of fellers in tow.

"King, I brung along a few o' my friends to help you and your'n celebrate this big day. I hope ye don't mind."

"You know I don't care a bit to have 'em here, 'Postle Jack," says the King. "Any friend o' yours is welcome at my home and to my table."

"Thank ye, King," says 'Postle Jack. "But did we miss the ceremony already? I don't see the preacher anywheres."

"Well, 'Postle Jack, I tell ye," says the King. "That preacher was coming a fair piece and I hear, with all this rain we been havin' ourselves, the creek has rised up and blocked the road. I'm afraid that preacher jes' may not be comin'."

"That don't make no never mind, King," says 'Postle Jack. "We kin marry them kids off proper without a preacher man sayin' no special words, sure."

"Well, that ain't all of it, 'Postle Jack," says the King. "We only got half the feast we planned on having, on account o' the rain comin' through the roof of the pantry and spoiling most o' what was prepared. And I had done hired the Muddy Bottom Boys to come and play for this here shindig, and they cain't git 'cross the creek neither."

"King, you jes' go ahead as you intended," says 'Postle Jack, "and I'll see what I kin do."

So the King hollered for everybody what was there to gather under the tent at one end. Then he called out Little John, who came out looking as nervous as a cat on a porch full of rockers, all dressed up in his go to meetin' suit. Next, the King called out Kelly Jo, and when she showed herself, all decked out in her mama's white lace courting dress, everybody what was there gasped in wonderment at how beautiful she looked. When Kelly Jo and Little John were standing there together with the King, in front of all their neighbors and kin, 'Postle Jack stepped forward.

"Now folks," says 'Postle Jack, "I ain't a preacher, that's sure as certain. But I know that when two young'uns love each other the way these two do, why, it don't take a preacher to marry them. Now, Kelly Jo and John Daniel, (that bein' Little John's proper name and all), bein' married isn't something you do all of a once't; it's something that happens over a lifetime o' sharing moments together, good ones and bad ones. These two young'uns are gonna have days filled with joy and laughter, that's certain. They're also gonna have their share o' days filled with sadness and tears. Now, how they make it through them days is gonna be their business, and nobody has a right to say anything about how they do it. But, if'n they vow to make it through those days, both good and bad, together, the two of 'em, then that's what bein' married is. Now, what we're doin' here," says 'Postle Jack, looking out over all the gathered fold around, "this ain't the being married I been talking about. This is a wedding, and that's something altogether different. That's s'posed to be a celebration, full o' all the joy and laughter we kin manage to surround these two young'uns with. So we're gonna git to celebratin' jes' as soon as ever we kin."

Just then all the people cheered, and Kelly Jo burst out in a smile, and Little John forgot hisself, swooped up his bride and kissed her. But the King looked at 'Postle Jack with a look of concern on his face.

"We ain't got enough food for all these good folk, 'Postle Jack," says the King, "on account o' the rain and all."

"Don't ye fret none, King," says 'Postle Jack. "Look."

One by one, the guests at the celebration were coming forward, bringing with them all sorts of good things to eat. One old mother brung up two large loaves of fresh bread, and with them she brung a pound of flour. She set the bread on the table and the flour on the ground below. A young couple, neighbors of Kelly Jo, brung up a fresh-baked rhubarb pie, and two jars of rhubarb jam to boot. The pie went on the table, and the jam went next to the flour. Next came a delicious apple stack cake and a bushel of apples. Then came a casserole of shucky beans, and two jars of them same beans put up, and a plate of cornbread and a pound of cornmeal, and so on, until that table was laid out with a wonderful feast fit for the King's son and his bride. The pounding beneath the table would keep that couple in vittles for a good while to come too.

"Now, King," says 'Postle Jack, "no weddin' feast would be complete without music, that's certain. I ain't one o' them fancy players like the Muddy Bottom boys, but I'd be willin' to play my dulcimer for ye, if'n you care to hear it."

"That would be right nice, 'Postle Jack," says the King, smiling.

'Postle Jack took his dulcimer off his back and began to play a tune. And soon as ever he put pick to string, them other fellers what come with him, they began to dig out from somewheres all sorts of musical instruments. One strummed a banjo, and one began sawing on his fiddle. Pretty soon, a band of musicians entire was playing and the folks was setting to enjoy that wedding feast. Them players played all night long, and them folks ate and danced til the sun began to peek over the mountaintops at dawn.

John Daniel and Kelly Jo turned to face the sunrise, a new day to start a new way of life together, smiles on their faces and joy in their hearts. The King turned to thank 'Postle Jack for all he done to help these two young'uns start their life together, but 'Postle Jack weren't nowheres to be found. About that time, the preacher arrived and made sure that the marriage was all performed legal like. And soon as the preacher spoke his last words, the Muddy Bottom Boys showed up and set to playing too. Them folks all stayed on, celebrating through the day, and for all I know, they's still celebrating that joy. Leastwise, that's what they were doing last I heard tell of it.

'Postle Jack Wears a Path

———⇒►●◄⇐———

A man had a fig tree planted in his vineyard;
and he came looking for fruit on it…
(Luke 13:6)

———⇒►●◄⇐———

This here is the story of how 'Postle Jack showed some folks how to walk the path and lift their spirits all at the same time. It weren't what he did or how he walked what showed them folks the path, but them what was looking, they found it just the same. It happened like this.

'Postle Jack never was known to be what you might call a farmer or even a expert gardener, but he seemed to have a way with growing things: plants and animals and people. Folks was always asking 'Postle Jack's advice on how to care for their gardens and how you might could get pole beans to grow taller or tomatoes to grow juicier, and 'Postle Jack would do what he could to help them out best as he knew how. Well, one day, of a morning early, three sisters were sitting on the porch, talking about how they always wanted one of them fancy gardens in their yards, filled with lush green plants and brightly colored flowers and gentle trees for shade, and maybe a path for walking and a bench for sitting. About that time, 'Postle Jack wandered by and waved up at the three sisters.

"Mornin' to you'uns," says 'Postle Jack to the sisters as he starts to pass on by.

"Oh, 'Postle Jack," calls out the youngest of the sisters. "We're jes' setting here dreaming of gardens we wisht we could grow. If you've a word o' help, we'd be right pleased to hear it of you."

'Postle Jack stopped walking and turned to the sister what had spoken out to him. "I'd be right pleased to do what I kin to help you," he says, "though I ain't got much of what you'd call a green thumb. I'll be along directly to each of you'uns' houses and see if'n there's anything what I kin offer."

"Thank ye, 'Postle Jack," says the youngest sister to him, waving to him as he headed up the road.

Well, those three sisters hurried off each to her own house to prepare for 'Postle Jack's visit. It weren't long before 'Postle Jack walked up onto the porch of the oldest sister's house and commenced to knocking on the door.

"Oh, 'Postle Jack," says the oldest sister, "thank ye for stopping, but everything what I might care to know about my garden I can find out for myself. I have a whole stack of books about gardens, right next to my back door. And I have mail catalogues what I can order all sorts of plants from that will make my garden the prettiest folks have ever seen. So, as you kin see, I have no need of any words from you."

"That's fine, ma'am," says 'Postle Jack and he turns and heads on his way.

It weren't but a few minutes before 'Postle Jack was standing on the doorstep of the middle sister, knocking to wake the dead. As she opens the door, this sister says, "I am so pleased you're here, 'Postle Jack. Come in and set a spell." She shows him to the kitchen table where she has fresh blackberries and cream set out. 'Postle Jack helps hisself to the food and listens while this sister tells what she hopes her garden will look like. "I'm in the garden club, of course, and all the ladies will want to come and see what kinds of flowers and sech I grow in my garden." When 'Postle Jack had eaten his fill of them sweet blackberries, he says to the woman, "Now, sister, you wait here while I go into your garden, and I'll return directly." So, the woman sat and waited and 'Postle Jack toiled in the garden for the rest of the morning. When he finally returned to the woman's kitchen he told her what to do.

"Now, sister," says 'Postle Jack, "I done walked a small path through your garden, with curves and turns and what not. Every day, of a morning, go out into your garden and walk that path. Each time you come to a turn, stop and say right out loud, 'Grow, garden, grow!' If'n you do jes' what I say, soon your garden will be pretty as a field in the sunshine."

"Why, thank ye, 'Postle Jack," says the sister, and she waved as he headed out the door and on his way.

Soon, 'Postle Jack found hisself on the doorstep of the youngest sister, the one what had first called out to him. Even before he could commence to knocking, the door flew open and the woman burst out, her face beaming with delight.

"Oh, 'Postle Jack, I'm so thankful you are here," says the youngest sister, and she leads him to the kitchen table all set with fresh warm bread and a jar of rhubarb jam. While 'Postle Jack helped hisself to the fare what was set out, the woman told him how she always dreamed of having a garden in her yard, "a place what would be a genuine place o' rest and renewal for those what found theirselves in it," she says.

When 'Postle Jack had eaten his fill of bread and jam, he says to the woman, "Now sister, you wait here while I go into your garden, and I'll return directly." So she sat and waited and 'Postle Jack toiled in the garden for the long hours of the afternoon. When he finally returned to the woman's kitchen he told her what to do.

"Now, sister," says 'Postle Jack, "I done walked a small path through your garden, with curves and turns and what not. Every day, of a morning, go out into your garden and walk that path. Each time you come to a turn, stop and say right out loud, 'Grow, garden, grow!' If'n you do jes' what I say, soon your garden will be pretty as a forest at sunset."

"Why, thank ye, 'Postle Jack," says the youngest sister, and she waved as he headed out the door and on his way.

Well, days passed and the oldest sister read her books and looked through her catalogues and made her plans for her garden. But soon she lost interest and never came to plant anything in her yard at all.

The middle sister, at first, was very careful to do just exactly what 'Postle Jack had told her to do. The first morning she walked the path through her garden. At each turn, she stopped and said out loud, "Grow, garden, grow!" On the second and third mornings, she did the same. But on the fourth morning, she was busy in the house, and she didn't get to walk the path through her garden until almost noon. On the fifth day, she again walked in the morning and at every turn spoke out, "Grow, garden, grow." But, she felt a little silly talking out loud to the plants, like they were wayward young'uns in need of a switching. The sixth day, she slept late and completely forgot to walk the path in her garden. On the seventh day, the woman had to go into town in the morning, so she walked the path that evening when she finished her chores. On the eighth day and ninth day, the woman again walked the path in the morning and did just as 'Postle Jack had told her. But on the next day, she was in a hurry, so she walked quickly and didn't bother to stop and say "Grow, garden, grow" even one time. For the next five days, the woman just stood at her kitchen door and looked out over her garden and called out with a small sigh, "Please grow." After that, the woman gave up walking the path and talking to the garden at all, and since her garden did not grow, she told all her friends in the garden club that 'Postle Jack was really a liar and not to be believed.

Now the youngest sister, she followed 'Postle Jack's instructions exactly. Each morning, without fail, she went into the garden and walked the path 'Postle Jack had worn for her. At each turn, she stopped and bent down to whisper to the ground, "Grow, garden, grow!" Sometimes she would just stand at a turn in the path for a while watching the garden, wondering if the plants would really grow, just as 'Postle Jack had said. Day after day, she repeated her routine, and day after day, she would stop at each turn in the path and watch her garden.

After about two weeks of doing this, she spied the face of a young girl staring over the fence at her. The woman just walked the path, as she always did, and when she stopped and said, "Grow, garden, grow," the tow-headed young'un giggled.

"Why are you talkin' to your plants?" asks the girl.

"I'm encouraging them to grow up big and strong," says the woman. "What's your name, honey?"

"I'm Mary Alice," says the girl.

"My name is Sophie," says the woman.

"Pleased to meet you, Miss Sophie."

"Mary Alice, do you want to help me?"

"Oh, can I?" she says, delight in her eyes.

"Why sure, honey. I'd be right pleased to have you walk the path with me."

So Mary Alice and Sophie walked the garden path together, stopping at each turn and saying together, "Grow, garden, grow!"

"Why, Mary Alice, look how dry the ground looks right here," says Sophie at one turn.

"I'll fetch a pitcher of water, Miss Sophie," says Mary Alice, and in the wink of an eye she runs off to get the pitcher and carry water to every corner of the garden.

The next morning, when Sophie peered out of her back door, there was Mary Alice waiting to walk with her.

"I think we need to pull up some of these weeds, today," says Sophie to Mary Alice as they stopped at the first turn along the path. At each turn, after they pulled up all the weeds they could see, the two spoke out to the plants, "Grow, garden, grow!" And Mary Alice giggled.

The next morning, Sophie brought out her shears. "Good morning, Mary Alice," she says, greeting her young friend. "Today, I think we need to cut back some of them plants what are getting too tall and spindly."

As they pruned, Mary Alice looked down at the ground. "Oh, this way, all the little flowers can git their share o' sunshine too!" she says. And she bent her face to the flowers and blew them kisses.

Sophie and Mary Alice walked the garden path every day for weeks, and soon the garden was bright with color. One day, Mary Alice showed up with another child. "Miss Sophie, this is my friend, Emily. Can she walk the path with us today?"

"Why sure, honey," says Sophie. "You can bring Emily and any other of your friends what want to walk in our garden any ol' time. That's why it's here." The two girls jumped and giggled and ran down the path, stopping at each turn, shouting "Grow, garden, grow," and running on to the next turn in the path.

Each day, more and more children came to walk the path in the garden. "I git to carry the pitcher," says Mary Alice. "And I git to pull the weeds," says Emily. "And I git to cut with the cutters," says a little boy with hair the color of the stones along the path.

Other children were standing at each turn in the path, shouting out in their little voices, "C'mon, you little plants, grow up now!" Sophie smiled at the young'uns and watched them playing in the garden, and her soul seemed as full as it had ever been.

"Miss Sophie," says Mary Alice to her, of a sudden. "Can I bring my daddy to walk our path?"

"Why, you sure can, honey," says Sophie.

The next day, Mary Alice showed up with her daddy in tow, and walked him through the garden, stopping at each turn, pointing to the hostas and the peonies, showing him how to call out, "Grow, garden, grow!" When they reached the end of the path, the King (for that was Mary Alice's daddy) spoke right out to Sophie.

"Miss Sophie," says the King, "this here is the prettiest garden path I've walked in, law, ages. Do ye mind if I tell others 'bout this here place of beauty, so they can get their souls filled jes' as I have?"

"Why, King," says Sophie, "I don't care a bit to have you tell anybody you've a mind to tell of this here garden. Hit don't really belong to me; I just tend to it, with the help of all these young'uns ."

It weren't long before people from far and wide were coming to walk the path through Sophie's garden. Then one day 'Postle Jack happened by, and saw the garden filled with children and folks of every age, walking the path and sitting in the shade. Sophie spotted him and hurried over to his side.

"Oh, 'Postle Jack," she says, "look at what you made. Your garden has brung delight to so many souls."

"Hit ain't what I made," says 'Postle Jack to her. "I jes' wore a path; you tended the garden. You and them young'uns , I reckon," says 'Postle Jack, spying Mary Alice carrying a pitcher of water to a thirsty corner of the garden.

"Well, come walk the path with me, 'Postle Jack," says Sophie taking his arm.

"I'd be right pleased to do jes' that," says 'Postle Jack smiling and following after her.

For all I know, 'Postle Jack is still walking that path with Sophie. Leastwise, that's what he was doing, last time I heard tell of him.

'Postle Jack Sets a Light

———⇒►●◄⇐———

You are the light of the world. A city built on a hill cannot be hid.
No one after lighting a lamp puts it under the bushel basket,
but on the lampstand, and it gives light to all in the house.
Matthew 5:14-15

———⇒►●◄⇐———

Did I ever tell you about the time 'Postle Jack wandered away beyond the borders of the King's land, 'cross the big river into the low country? It seems 'Postle Jack found hisself looking off across the river, wondering if there might be some adventure of some sort waiting for him there. So, one day 'Postle Jack jumped on the ferry boat and rode across the big river from one bank to the other.

As soon as he'd crossed that muddy water, why he knew right away that he was in a different kind of country. For one thing, there weren't near as many mountains, almost none at all to speak of. Overlooking the banks of the muddy river rose a high bluff. Well, 'Postle Jack scrambled up that bluff, and he cast his eyes out in front of him; from there the land stretched away to the horizon in the west, with nothing but sky to stop it. A far piece in the distance, he could see what looked like neat little rows of growing things, too high and straight to be tobacco. 'Postle Jack took notice that all around him, on the edge of the bluff, were what seemed to be pieces of wood, splinters, burned logs, and glass and tar paper, almost in a pile, but with weeds and trees growing up through them. Running down the bluff toward the fields in the distance was a weedy path, that looked like nobody had traveled it for a long while. So 'Postle Jack took hisself down the path to see where it might lead him.

Well, it weren't long before 'Postle Jack spied a small cabin off from the path a ways. In the yard was a tired-looking woman, sweeping the dirt. Up on the porch were two dusty children playing with sticks and a bit of string. 'Postle Jack walked right on up to the woman's porch and spoke out to her.

"Mornin', Mother," 'Postle Jack says.

"Well, stranger," says the woman, "what kin I do for ye?"

"You kin pass me a cup o' water, if'n you've a mind to," says 'Postle Jack. "I've been walking a spell, and I'm powerful thirsty."

"A cup o' water we kin surely spare ye," says the woman, leading 'Postle Jack over to the well beside the porch, "but I'm afraid we don't have nary a scrap of food to offer ye, sir. Not even a strap of jerky to toss your way."

"How's that, mother?" asks 'Postle Jack, taking the cup of water from the woman's outstretched hand.

"Well, we don't have enough to shake a stick at," says the woman, "but what we had, I gave it to them young'uns and they et the last scrap this mornin'. My husband is out looking for a job o' work so's we kin buy what we need, but hit don't seem that there's work to be found, even for one that's willing."

'Postle Jack reached into the bag on his back and pulled out a few stale biscuits and what was left of a jar of rhubarb jam. "Here, Mother," he says, handing them to the woman. "These is for your young'uns, jes til your husband gits home with supplies."

"Thank ye, kindly, sir," the woman says. "You're welcome in our home anytime."

'Postle Jack waved to the children as he headed back down the path. It weren't long before he came upon what he took to be a stump in the middle of the road, but soon discovered it was a bent-over old man, resting from the heat of the day with his hat down over his face.

"Grandfather," says 'Postle Jack to the old man, "kin you tell me if'n there's a town anywhere's along this road?"

"Why, sure as certain, there is, stranger," says the old man, looking out at 'Postle Jack from under the brim of his hat. "Hit ain't but another small piece down the road. Go past two houses, a great cornfield, and a big red barn. Then, the road turns to the right, and in another bit you'll find yourself right smack in the middle of town."

"Thank ye, Grandfather," says 'Postle Jack, as he starts on his way.

"But I'd go back the other way, if'n I was you," says the old man.

"Why's that?"

"Well, that town don't exactly welcome strangers. They's busy with their own affairs, and they hain't got no use fer strangers and old folks and the like, nobody 'cept them what kin make their own way and not be a trouble to their neighbor," says the old man. "If'n you kin even call 'em that," he adds, spitting in the dirt next to where he was sitting.

"I thank ye fer your words, Grandfather," says 'Postle Jack, and he set off again down the road, wondering what could of caused a town full of people to end up the way this old man was saying it.

Just like the old man had said, 'Postle Jack soon found hisself wandering past them two houses, and a cornfield with the greenest, tallest, straightest corn he ever did lay eyes on. He passed the big red barn too, but nowheres did he see a soul, nor did nary a voice call out to him in greeting. It was getting on to be late in the day when 'Postle Jack finally found hisself in the middle of town, the bank on one side and the courthouse on the other, but they both looked locked up tight, to keep out strangers sure as likely. Down the street a ways 'Postle Jack finally spied a boardinghouse with a sign "Rooms to Rent" in the front window. He marched hisself up onto the porch and commenced to knocking on the door. Pretty soon, a sad-looking man come to the door.

"What kin I do fer ye, stranger?" says the man to 'Postle Jack.

"Well, I'm needin' a room to stay in fer a spell, and I was hopin' you'd be willin' to have me stay in one a your'n."

"I don't care a bit to have you here," says the man, and he opens the door and shows 'Postle Jack into the kitchen, where a fresh pitcher of cold tea is setting next to a couple tall glasses and a peach pie. The innkeeper poured out some tea for 'Postle Jack. "Sit down, stranger," says the man, "and tell me how you came to be in our town."

So 'Postle Jack told him how he had traveled across the muddy river on the ferry, and how he had come over the bluff and down the path and found his way.

"That's the path from the old church meetinghouse," says the man, a sad look in his eyes. "Time was, we used to travel that path ourselves, ever' one, man, woman, and child, of a Sunday afternoon, when the work on the farms was done, at least enough for a Sunday. Each family'd pack them up a mess o' food and make their way up the path. Neighbors would sing and wave to each other and nobody was a stranger. Others would join along the way, til there was a right fair crowd climbing up to the edge of the bluff there for Sunday Meeting. Then, we'd have singin' and prayin' and preachin' in the cool of the evening, and after, we'd have dinner on the grounds. Then, as night began to fall, folks would pack up and sing a final song before settin' off, each to their own homes."

"What happened?" asks 'Postle Jack, taking his second piece of pie from the plate and drenching it with sweet cream from the pitcher.

"Well, 'bout four years ago, the church house was struck by lightning and burnt to the ground," the man says with a sigh. "Since that day, we ain't had even one Sunday Meeting. Folks have jes' seemed to go their own way, what with bein' so busy and all. And there jes' didn't seem to be any point to it after a time."

The next morning, 'Postle Jack was up at sunrise, pacing up and down the porch and looking up the road out of town, back toward the bluff. Right soon, the innkeeper come out onto the porch.

"What're you doin' up so early, Son? And you're gonna wear out my floorboards and my patience with all that pacing!" says the innkeeper with a sigh. "Why don't you come on inside and I'll fix you a pot o' coffee and a plate o' buttermilk pancakes with sausage."

"That'd be right good," says 'Postle Jack. "But then, I got a task I'm gonna need some help with. You know any fellers what might need a job o' work round here?"

"There's allus a few fellers settin' on the courthouse steps of a mornin', lookin' for a job o' work," says the innkeeper. "But mostly, they just sit there, and nobody hires 'em."

As soon as ever as 'Postle Jack ate his fill of them pancakes, though, he was off to the courthouse, where he found three fellers who were willing to help him with his task. "Now, I ain't got no money to pay you with," says 'Postle Jack to the fellers.

"That's fine with us," says one feller. "We much prefer workin' to settin' all day feelin' useless."

First thing he does, 'Postle Jack sets them fellers to find some tall trees to cut. "They gotta be sturdy trees, fellers," says 'Postle Jack, "to make sturdy logs."

As soon as them fellers were set on their way, 'Postle Jack hurries back up the road to the top of the bluff, and busies hisself all day long up there. Pretty soon, the people in the town began to notice 'Postle Jack walking back and forth up there on the edge of the bluff, dragging and carrying and doing Lord only knows what. Then, them fellers come through town with a wagonload of felled trees cut into sturdy logs, heading up the road toward the bluff. By the end of the day, curiosity got the best of them, and a whole passel of farmers and townsfolk were standing on the edge of the bluff, staring at 'Postle Jack and the three other fellers.

Finally, someone spoke out. "What're you up to, stranger?" says a man with a wrinkled face.

"Why, cain't you tell?" says 'Postle Jack. "We're building a church meetinghouse. And we could use some more help."

"Well, I'd be right pleased to help," says one feller.

"I'll do whatever I kin," says one woman, brushing her hands on her apron.

Soon, almost all those folks were saying as how they'd be willing to lend a hand too. The next day, 'Postle Jack had them folks carrying logs and buckets and brushes and brooms up the road to the edge of the bluff. Those what remembered going to Sunday Meeting at the old church meetinghouse on the bluff, they were the most eager to work. Others, those what had never been to Sunday Meeting there, they lagged behind, sighing and complaining a bit in the heat of the day. But at the end of the day, when the work come to a stop, the folks lingered in the town square between the bank and the courthouse. Some told stories of Sunday Meetings they recalled. Others sang hymns they recollected singing. Still others talked of the dinners on the grounds they used to have after Sunday Meeting, and all the good food: the corn on the cob slathered in sweet butter, cold steaks that had been cooked over a slow fire, tangy potato salad, German chocolate cake, and huge pitchers of cold tea and lemonade. As the days went by, the work went quickly and soon the folks had built a log meetinghouse up on the edge of the bluff, overlooking the great muddy river to the east and the cornfields to the west. The last thing to be carried up the road was the old church bell that had been salvaged from the fire and kept in the big red barn just outside of town. 'Postle Jack hung that bell on a sturdy post in the front yard of the church meetinghouse, and rang it loud, just to make sure it worked. All them people stopped what they was doing and turned to listen to 'Postle Jack.

"Now, it's Saturday, folks. Tomorrow, of a evenin', let's have us a Sunday Meeting," says 'Postle Jack.

"And dinner on the grounds," says the woman with the apron. "We'll all carry in ever what we got to share."

Folks were agreeing, saying as how that sounds right nice and all. Then the man with the wrinkled face says, "How are we gonna have Sunday Meeting in this here church house, 'Postle Jack. Hit ain't got no 'lectricity to see by."

'Postle Jack smiled and called out toward the church meetinghouse. The doors swung wide and a passel of children came out, carrying jelly jar lanterns. "Now, there's a lantern here for each family in town," says 'Postle Jack. "You'uns need to bring your lantern here to the Sunday Meeting, so your light kin shine with others. If'n you don't bring your light, your corner of the church house will be dark." The children gave each family one of those jelly jar lanterns, and folks set on their way home to get ready for the next day.

Long about sundown that Sunday, 'Postle Jack stood on the bluff looking out over the town, and commenced to ringing that old church bell in the meetinghouse yard. And this is what he seen. Folks commenced to pouring out of their farms and houses, from fields and town, each family carrying a lantern in front of them. It were like little trickles of light running through the countryside, until they all came together in one great river of light, running up the road toward the church on the bluff. All them people started pouring into the church meetinghouse, and their lanterns filled that place to overflowing. The old man who was setting in the road before, he was down by the river, and when he looked up to the edge of the bluff, he saw that light shining from the church house. So he made his way up the bluff and found hisself being welcomed into the meeting. The woman with the two children, she saw all them lights pass by her house going up the road, and she grabbed her young'uns and followed, until she found herself sitting in the back of the church meetinghouse, singing and praying with the rest of them. The children were on the floor in the back, eating a big plate of potato casserole that the woman with the apron had served out for them. Soon, the church meetinghouse was filled with light enough to shine out over the fields and down the bluff to the banks of the muddy river below.

When the folks were finished singing and praying and preaching, and they was all set to have dinner on the grounds, someone asked, "Why, where's 'Postle Jack? We need to thank him fer his help." Everyone set to looking for him, but he was nowheres to be found. At last, one of the children cried out and pointed down the bluff. When the people came and looked down, they saw floating in the water below, two wooden beams in the shape of a cross, with jelly jar lanterns burning bright all along their length.

The folks never knew what happened to 'Postle Jack after that; he was off to find his next adventure. But ever after that, every Sunday evening those people stopped what they was doing and lit their jelly jar lanterns and made their way to the church on the bluff, where there was singing and praying and preaching, and dinner on the grounds. And all what was lonely were satisfied. And all what was hungry were filled. And all what was looking for a job of work was hired, and all what was in need of something found what they were needing there in the light of the church on the bluff. And every Sunday, just after the sun goes down over the fields, if you look up across the river toward the top of the bluff, you'll see a great light shining for everyone to see. And there ain't never been a dark corner since 'Postle Jack set that light to shining. Leastwise, that's the way I heard it.

For Further Reflection

This section is a companion to the 'Postle Jack Tales. You will find the titles of each story, followed by a scripture reference to one of the four gospels (sometimes edited for clarity). After each scripture passage, there is a brief reflection that I hope will serve as a way of beginning to bring the Biblical text and the 'Postle Jack Tale into dialogue with one another and with your experience. These reflections are only meant to serve as a starting point in the conversation, not as an exhaustive or definitive summary. It is my hope that these reflections would lead you deeper into the scriptures and back to the 'Postle Jack Tales, until you are able to discern for yourself where the grace is to be found in each and how the reign of God is envisioned in each. As you begin to answer those questions for yourself, I know that the parables and stories from scripture will speak to you of God's overwhelming grace. I also hope that these reflections will open up new layers of meaning and insight for you as you revisit 'Postle Jack's world again and again.

———————➤●◄———————

'Postle Jack Makes a Promise
Luke 1:5-14, 57-58, 80

"In the days of King Herod of Judea, there was a priest named Zechariah. His wife was Elizabeth. Both of them were righteous before God, but they had no children, because Elizabeth was barren. Once when he was serving as priest before God, there appeared to Zechariah an angel of the Lord…. The angel said to him, 'Do not be afraid, Zechariah, for your prayer has been heard. Your wife Elizabeth will bear you a son, and you will name him John. You will have joy and gladness, and many will rejoice at his birth.' Now the time came for Elizabeth to give birth, and she bore a son. Her neighbors and relatives heard that the Lord had shown his great mercy to her, and they rejoiced with her. The child grew and became strong in spirit."

God often works through prophetic promises spoken by messengers. Those promises take root in us and grow hopes and dreams and expectations. They have a way of lingering in our souls, until they shape us into the people God would have us become. At least, that seems to be what happened to Zechariah and Elizabeth and John. An old couple hears a prophetic promise about their child from a holy messenger, and hopes and dreams and expectations begin to form for their son and for their people and for their nation. Then, sure enough, John grows up and fulfills every one of those hopes and dreams and expectations, as he becomes the person God would have him be. I wonder how much that prophetic promise really shaped the hopes and dreams and expectations of Zechariah and Elizabeth, so that they nurtured John on them as he grew, until he ultimately fulfilled them. How much are children shaped into who they become by the hopes and dreams and expectations we have for them? How much are our children nurtured on the prophetic promise we hold up for them to fulfill? That's the way God works.

'Postle Jack and the Bean Pickers
Matthew 20:1-16

"For the kingdom of heaven is like a landowner who went out early in the morning to hire laborers for his vineyard. After agreeing with the laborers for the usual daily wage, he sent them into his vineyard. When he went out about nine o'clock, he saw others standing idle in the marketplace; and he said to them, 'You also go into the vineyard, and I will pay you whatever is right.' So they went. When he went out again about noon and about three o'clock, he did the same. And about five o'clock he went out and found others standing around; and he said to them, 'Why are you standing here idle all day?' They said to him, 'Because no one has hired us.' He said to them, 'You also go into the vineyard.' When evening came, the owner of the vineyard said to his manager, 'Call the laborers and give them their pay, beginning with the last and then going to the first.' When those hired about five o'clock came, each of them received the usual daily wage. Now when the first came, they thought they would receive more; but each of them also received the usual daily wage. And when they received it, they grumbled against the landowner, saying, 'These last worked only one hour, and you have made them equal to us who have borne the burden of the day and the scorching heat.' But he replied to one of them, 'Friend, I am doing you no wrong; did you not agree with me for the usual daily wage? Take what belongs to you and go; I choose to give to this last the same as I give to you. Am I not allowed to do what I choose with what belongs to me? Or are you envious because I am generous?' So the last will be first, and the first will be last."

How often do we wonder what heaven must be like: are there streets paved with gold, perhaps, or choirs of angels singing magnificently, or maybe it's fields and flowers, meadows and mountains, sparkling streams and gentle breezes? Maybe your image of heaven isn't about places and things at all, but people and relationships: being reunited with loved ones, a life without struggle or pain or loneliness.

Whatever your vision of heaven may be, it is for you a comforting vision, one that you take pleasure in contemplating.

Oh, how different is the vision of the kingdom of heaven in Matthew's gospel. Over and over again, Matthew introduces us to the kingdom of heaven with parables and metaphors that shock and disturb. Matthew recounts parables in which the kingdom of heaven is compared to a weed, to mold, and to a vengeful king who punishes unforgiving servants. Now, here, Matthew puts forth a wholly unpleasant vision of the kingdom of heaven; unpleasant at least for us who live in the culture of western North American capitalism. We hear this parable and it disturbs us, because it calls into question all our most fundamental understandings about justice, and fairness, and human relationships, and even God's grace. It questions our uniquely American ideal of pulling ourselves up by our own bootstraps. It questions our notion that if you work hard and live a just and honest life, you will get ahead and be duly rewarded. It challenges our completely nonbiblical maxim, "God helps those who help themselves." It challenges our competitive view of the world; if somebody is going to win, somebody else has to lose. It clearly tells us that life in the kingdom of heaven is not anything like our life here: it is a radically different way of living and treating each other, a way that is characterized by justice and grace.

———————

'Postle Jack at Trouble Creek
Matthew 21:33-41, 43

Jesus said, "Listen to another parable. There was a landowner who planted a vineyard, put a fence around it, dug a wine press in it, and built a watchtower. Then he leased it to tenants and went to another country. When the harvest time had come, he sent his slaves to the tenants to collect his produce. But the tenants seized his slaves and beat one, killed another, and stoned another. Again he sent other slaves, more than the first; and they treated them in the same way. Finally he sent his son to them, saying, 'They will respect my son.' But when the tenants saw the son, they said to themselves, 'This is the heir; come, let us kill him and get his inheritance.' So they seized him, threw him out of the vineyard, and killed him. Now when the owner of the vineyard comes, what will he do to those tenants?"

They said to him, "He will put those wretches to a miserable death, and lease the vineyard to other tenants who will give him the produce at the harvest time."

Jesus said to them, "Therefore I tell you, the kingdom of God will be taken away from you and given to a people that produces the fruits of the kingdom."

How is the Kingdom of God like tenant laborers who beat and kill servants, even kill the landowner's son, thinking they will inherit what isn't theirs to own in the first place? How is the harsh judgment Jesus' listeners pronounce on these people any comfort to us as we search longingly for a word of Grace to bless our spirits? How can we not hear in this story the fearful presence of evil and the terrible sin of self-condemnation that hangs like a stone around our shoulders weighing down our souls?

Sometimes we take for granted all the blessings we have been given. We are so used to living surrounded on all sides by God's grace that we forget how really miraculous it is! We fall into a pattern in our lives and we start seeing where we have failed, instead of seeing the successes that have carried us this far. We look around us and we see all the things we don't have, instead of seeing the abundance of riches showered on us. We spend our days with family and friends, yet we mourn those who are gone, relationships we have lost, friends and lovers who have left us, instead of rejoicing in the richness of the loving relationships of those who stand beside us day after day. If we let it, our logic can become flawed, and we can begin to think we are those most cursed of all God's people, forgotten, neglected, oppressed, kept out of the sunshine for far too many years. Instead of approaching God with grateful hearts, we complain to God with angry souls. We begin to wall ourselves in, trusting nobody, expecting little, giving nothing, and our home becomes a wilderness of our own design. When that happens, sometimes it takes something shocking, something scandalous, something miraculous to bring us back to the place where God wants us to dwell.

There is no corner of God's world that is too far removed to be forgotten by God. And there is no trouble so great that it can separate us from the saving grace God has waiting for us. And we are never so far from God that our needs are not already known and waiting to be given to us.

———◈———

'Postle Jack and the Invitation
Matthew 22:2-14

"The kingdom of heaven may be compared to a king who gave a wedding banquet for his son. He sent his slaves to call those who had been invited to the wedding banquet, but they would not come. Again he sent other slaves, saying, 'Tell those who have been invited: Look, I have prepared my dinner, my oxen and my fat calves have been slaughtered, and everything is ready; come to the wedding banquet.' But they made light of it and went away, one to his farm, another to his business, while the rest seized his slaves, mistreated them, and killed them. The king was enraged. He sent his troops, destroyed those murderers, and burned their city. Then he said to his slaves, 'The wedding is ready, but those invited were not worthy. Go therefore into the main streets, and invite everyone you find to the wedding banquet.' Those slaves went out into the streets and gathered all whom they found, both good and bad; so the wedding hall was filled with guests.

But when the king came in to see the guests, he noticed a man there who was not wearing a wedding robe, and he said to him, 'Friend, how did you get in here without a wedding robe?' And he was speechless. Then the king said to the attendants, 'Bind him hand and foot, and throw him into the outer darkness, where there will be weeping and gnashing of teeth.' For many are called, but few are chosen."

The Kingdom of Heaven isn't some faraway place and some yet-to-be time. The Kingdom of Heaven is now, and it is like being invited to a celebration. The celebration is life and everybody is invited to participate. How you respond to that invitation is up to you. It's not about what kinds of clothes you wear, or how you look, or what your station is in life. It's about how you approach the life you've been invited to share with those around you. Some people seem to pass through life like it's an obligation. Some people seem too busy with other things to join the celebration going on around them. And some people are just downright mean. By their own choices, these people have already banished themselves to dwell in outer darkness, away from the light of life and the joy of celebration. But then there are those people who know what an honor it is to receive an invitation from the King, those who are overjoyed that we have been invited to this celebration called life. And we clean ourselves up and put on our best and we join the celebration with everything we have, not out of obligation, but out of gratitude. And when we come to the celebration, we find ourselves entertained, fed, emotionally satisfied, spiritually filled, and joyfully received.

The Kingdom of Heaven isn't just about what heaven will be like when we get there at some future time. It's about how we live our lives now, and how we approach each other, and why we do the things we do, and how we respond to the presence of God's grace breaking into our lives every day, whether with joy out of a sense of gratitude or with reluctance out of a sense of obligation.

———⟫●⟪———

'Postle Jack Haints a Town
Luke 10:25-37

Just then a lawyer stood up to test Jesus. "Teacher," he said, "what must I do to inherit eternal life?" He said to him, "What is written in the law? What do you read there?" He answered, "You shall love the Lord your God with all your heart, and with all your soul, and with all your strength, and with all your mind; and your neighbor as yourself." And he said to him, "You have given the right answer; do this, and you will live."

But wanting to justify himself, he asked Jesus, "And who is my neighbor?" Jesus replied, "A man was going down from Jerusalem to Jericho, and fell into the hands of robbers, who stripped him, beat him, and went away, leaving him half dead. Now by chance a priest was going down that road; and when he saw him, he passed by on the other side. So likewise a Levite, when he came to the place and saw him, passed by on the other side. But a Samaritan while traveling came near him; and when he saw him, he was moved with pity. He went to him and bandaged his wounds, having poured oil and wine on them. Then he put him on his own animal, brought him to an inn, and took care of him. The next day he took out two denarii, gave them to the innkeeper, and said, 'Take care of him; and when I come back, I will repay you whatever more you spend.' Which of these three, do you think, was a neighbor to the man who fell into the hands of the robbers?" He said, "The one who showed him mercy." Jesus said to him, "Go and do likewise."

We think we know the answers, don't we? The answers have been around for millennia. The ancient Hebrews recited the answers as soon as Moses spoke them at the foot of the holy mountain. The Israelites of first century Judea knew them by heart and could recite them at the drop of a hat. We know the answers. Like the lawyer who talked with Jesus, we have learned the right answers; we even know how to ask the right questions. We can justify ourselves with the best of them. But when it comes to living the answers, somehow we seem to fall short.

In our present-day climate of fear and uncertainty, we allow our fears and hatreds of those who seem different from us to rule our behavior and limit our compassion. We avoid those who we think are less than perfect, those whose skin is a different color, those whose lifestyle is oriented differently, those whose social and economic status is below ours, those whose language we can't speak, those whose belief system is beyond our understanding. And then, like the lawyer, when we are confronted by the reality of the Living God calling us to live the answers we have learned, we hesitate, we argue, we question, we seek to justify, until there is nowhere left to hide from our own hatreds and prejudices that keep us from doing what we know God wants us to do.

We know what God wants from us; the lawyer's answers ring true in our ears: "You shall love the Lord your God with all your heart, and with all your soul, and with all your strength, and with all your mind; and your neighbor as yourself." We can assent to his answer, because we know it is the right answer. But we become uneasy when, wanting to justify himself, the lawyer asks, "And who is my neighbor?" It is this question that haunts us still, some twenty centuries later, and a world away.

'Postle Jack's Family Reunion
Matthew 25:1-13

"Then the kingdom of heaven will be like this. Ten bridesmaids took their lamps and went to meet the bridegroom. Five of them were foolish, and five were wise. When the foolish took their lamps, they took no oil with them; but the wise took flasks of oil with their lamps. As the bridegroom was delayed, all of them became drowsy and slept. But at midnight there was a shout, 'Look! Here is the bridegroom! Come out to meet him.' Then all those bridesmaids got up and trimmed their lamps. The foolish said to the wise, 'Give us some of your oil, for our lamps are going out.' But the wise replied, 'No! there will not be enough for you and for us; you had better go to the dealers and buy some for yourselves.' And while they went to buy it, the bridegroom came, and those who were ready went with him into the wedding banquet; and the door was shut. Later the other bridesmaids came also, saying, 'Lord, lord, open to us.' But he replied, 'Truly I tell you, I do not know you.' Keep awake, therefore, for you know neither the day nor the hour."

The whole notion of family reunions intrigues me. I guess it's because they seem so artificial. Why would a bunch of strangers who once had a common ancestor necessarily want to get together and spend time with each other, when they don't know each other from Adam? When some families have a reunion, everybody pretty much knows everybody else. But still, does that mean that just because they are kin, they have some kind of claim on each other, on their lives and time and attention, more so than the friends and neighbors they spend each and every day with? It seems to me that being family is about something a lot more complicated than whether or not your daddy and her momma are first cousins. Being family means caring about one another, being involved in the lives of each other, knowing what's going on with each other, praying for each other, liking each other, and loving each other. That doesn't happen by going to a reunion once every year or two. Building a relationship, establishing a kinship, takes a lifetime of effort. A relationship can't be built all at once, just when you need or want something; relationships don't just happen that way. A relationship is established, or not, by a thousand little moments every day and every night over a lifetime together.

We can't choose who we are related to by blood or by birth; but we do choose who we have relationships with by our actions and our lifestyles and our behaviors. And our choices have consequences. If we choose to ignore a kinship tie, that relationship withers and dies. If we choose to nurture a friendship or a family tie, that relationship grows and deepens and is enriched. Those with whom we choose to nurture relationships become our brothers and sisters, our family. It is among them we are welcomed home.

—————⇒⊱●⊰⇐—————

'Postle Jack Plants Some Seeds
Matthew 13:1-8

"That same day Jesus went out of the house and sat beside the sea. Such great crowds gathered around him that he got into a boat and sat there, while the whole crowd stood on the beach. And he told them many things in parables, saying: 'Listen! A sower went out to sow. And as he sowed, some seeds fell on the path, and the birds came and ate them up. Other seeds fell on rocky ground, where they did not have much soil, and they sprang up quickly, since they had no depth of soil. But when the sun rose, they were scorched; and since they had no root, they withered away. Other seeds fell among thorns, and the thorns grew up and choked them. Other seeds fell on good soil and brought forth grain, some a hundredfold, some sixty, some thirty.'"

Jesus told the same stories to everybody; he told them to the disciples and the Pharisees, to the tax collectors and to the scribes, to the lepers and to the rich young rulers. He told them stories, like a sower sowing seeds. The thing about stories, and parables, is that they have a way of lingering in your soul and growing there, like seeds planted in soil. Sometimes they wither and die. Sometimes these stories take root and grow, strong and straight, yielding a hundredfold in your life.

Jesus trusted that people would hear the stories and understand and that their lives would be changed. Jesus trusted that the kingdom of Heaven would begin to take root in the world, wherever people began to care for one another, whenever people treated each other like children of the King, wherever lives were guided by selfless love.

We are still telling the stories.

———⟫●⟪———

'Postle Jack Returns
Luke 15:11-32

Then Jesus said, "There was a man who had two sons. The younger of them said to his father, 'Father, give me the share of the property that will belong to me.' So he divided his property between them. A few days later the younger son gathered all he had and traveled to a distant country, and there he squandered his property in dissolute living. When he had spent everything, a severe famine took place throughout that country, and he began to be in need. So he went and hired himself out to one of the citizens of that country, who sent him to his fields to feed the pigs. He would gladly have filled himself with the pods that the pigs were eating; and no one gave him anything. But when he came to himself he said, 'How many of my father's hired hands have bread enough and to spare, but here I am dying of hunger! I will get up and go to my father, and I will say to him, 'Father, I have sinned against heaven and before you; I am no longer worthy to be called your son; treat me like one of your hired hands.' So he set off and went to his father. But while he was still far off, his father saw him and was filled with compassion; he ran and put his arms around him and kissed him. Then the son said to him, 'Father, I have sinned against heaven and before you; I am no longer worthy to be called your son.' But the father said to his slaves, 'Quickly, bring out a robe–the best one–and put it on him; put a ring on his finger and sandals on his feet. And get the fatted calf and kill it, and let us eat and celebrate; for this son of mine was dead and is alive again; he was lost and is found!' And they began to celebrate.

"Now his elder son was in the field; and when he came and approached the house, he heard music and dancing. He called one of the slaves and asked what was going on. He replied, 'Your brother has come, and your father has killed the fatted calf, because he has got him back safe and sound.' Then he became angry and refused to go in. His father came out and began to plead with him. But he answered his father, 'Listen! For all these years I have been working like a slave for you, and I have never disobeyed your command; yet you have never given me even a young goat so that I might celebrate with my friends.

But when this son of yours came back, who has devoured your property with prostitutes, you killed the fatted calf for him!' Then the father said to him, 'Son, you are always with me, and all that is mine is yours. But we had to celebrate and rejoice, because this brother of yours was dead and has come to life; he was lost and has been found.'"

One time at a youth conference, the kids were asked to say what the kingdom of God was like. They were coming up with all the usual answers, until one said, "I think the kingdom of God is always here; we just don't always show up." Jesus told stories that seemed to say the same thing. The story of the father and the two sons seems to be about a lot of things, but certainly it is about God's celebration and how we choose or don't choose to join that celebration of life.

In the reign of God, the table is always set, the stories are told, the songs are sung, and the celebration goes on. And at God's celebration, all of us are special, and there is enough for each one of us. When we refuse to show up, we punish ourselves and deny ourselves the joy of fellowship. But when we do show up, we discover what has been waiting for us, what has been prepared especially for us. When we show up we discover the blessings that have our name on them, that nobody else can take from us. The celebration is always here; we just don't always show up.

How 'Postle Jack Got His Call
Matthew 4:18-22

"As Jesus walked by the Sea of Galilee, he saw two brothers, Simon, who is called Peter, and Andrew his brother, casting a net into the sea— for they were fishermen. And he said to them, 'Follow me, and I will make you fish for people.' Immediately they left their nets and followed him. As he went from there, he saw two other brothers, James son of Zebedee, and his brother John, in the boat with their father, Zebedee, mending their nets, and he called them. Immediately they left the boat and their father, and followed him."

Miss Mattie was the woman who took care of all the little children at the church in Houston, Texas, where I was serving as youth minister. She had been there about twenty years and she knew every child by name, and every child knew her by name. She was a large, imposing woman, not somebody you would want to argue with, but she was also as sweet and gentle as she could be with those little children, offering them God's love in a way only Miss Mattie could do.

When I was preparing to leave that church to be pastor of a small church in Kentucky, the staff gave me a bible. Each person on the staff underlined a verse and wrote a note to me. Miss Mattie underlined John 3:16. Next to it she wrote, "I am so glad you got your call." When I first saw that, I thought to myself, "What does she mean? I got my call a long time ago, didn't I? What have I been doing for the past five years, if I'm just now getting my call?" After a while, though, I came to know what Miss Mattie meant.

Every call to discipleship isn't as clearly life-changing as the first disciples' call to follow Jesus. Sometimes, getting your call means simply responding to the urgings of the heart in a way that uses the gifts God has given you. Sometimes getting your call comes as a surprise at first, but you don't really recognize it until you are ready to seek it out and receive it. Like Andrew, Simon, James, and John, you have to be willing to seek out your call, and respond with your whole life, and follow faithfully, or you might waste a lot of time and effort serving in a way that may be good and faithful, but isn't your call. Once you start looking, and listening, for that thing that God most wants you to do with your life, your gifts and skills, that's when you are going to "get your call." But you have to be looking, and listening, and you have to be ready to respond with your life: heart, mind, and soul. Or you might just miss it.

What 'Postle Jack Gave
Matthew 25:14-27

"For it is as if a man, going on a journey, summoned his slaves and entrusted his property to them; to one he gave five talents, to another two, to another one, to each according to his ability. Then he went away. The one who had received the five talents went off at once and traded with them, and made five more talents. In the same way, the one who had the two talents made two more talents. But the one who had received the one talent went off and dug a hole in the ground and hid his master's money. After a long time the master of those slaves came and settled accounts with them. Then the one who had received the five talents came forward, bringing five more talents….And the one with the two talents also came forward, saying 'Master, you handed over to me two talents; see, I have made two more talents.'… Then the one who had received the one talent also came forward, saying, 'Master, I knew that you were a harsh man, reaping where you did not sow, and gathering where you did not scatter seed; so I was afraid, and I went and hid your talent in the ground. Here you have what is yours.' But his master replied, 'You wicked and lazy slave! You knew, did you, that I reap where I did not sow, and gather where I did not scatter? Then you ought to have invested my money with the bankers, and on my return I would have received what was my own with interest.'"

Sometimes I wonder what we really believe as a faith community. Does our market economy govern our lives, determining how we spend and how we save our financial resources? Or does our faith govern our lives, even our decisions about money, telling us that God wants us to live in a way that sees even financial spending as an enrichment of our world? Do we truly believe that we create more rather than use something up when we give of our time and self and resources? Do we trust that God will use what we offer to add joy and blessing and grace to the world? Or do we value only what we can accumulate and appraise? Do we truly consider our gifts of time and self and financial resources an investment, a means for building up God's world? Or do we consider it a spending program, emptying our pockets and our energies for some intangible purpose?

The grace of God is so much more than we can expect or imagine that sometimes it seems to come to us like magic, and we find it hard to believe, hard to trust, hard to accept. God blesses us with gifts, resources and abilities, and God wants us to enjoy the gifts we are given. Still, it is up to us to discover what gift God is giving and why God is giving that gift to us. Then it is up to us to receive the gift and determine how we shall use the gift. Are we willing and ready to use the gifts God has given us the way God intends us to use them? Or are we afraid to use them, to believe in them, to trust the grace of being gifted? If we use our gifts, will they be all used up? Are the gifts we have received really ours to decide when and how to use them? Or were they given to us to bring life and joy and hope to us and to the people around us?

—————>❖<—————

'Postle Jack in Paradise
Matthew 6:25-33

"Is not life more than food, and the body more than clothing? Look at the birds of the air; they neither sow nor reap nor gather into barns, and yet your heavenly Father feeds them. Are you not of more value than they? And can any of you by worrying add a single hour to your span of life? And why do you worry about clothing? Consider the lilies of the field, how they grow; they neither toil nor spin, yet I tell you, even Solomon in all his glory was not clothed like one of these. But if God so clothes the grass of the field, which is alive today and tomorrow is thrown into the oven, will he not much more clothe you— you of little faith…. But strive first for the kingdom of God and his righteousness, and all these things will be given to you as well."

Sometimes we get caught up in the worries of the world. Each day brings its challenges and makes demands of us. There are deadlines to meet, appointments to keep, bills to pay, obligations to fulfill. Sometimes we get so caught up in the chaos of daily life that we forget what is most valuable about life. We begin to equate our worth with our earning potential or our achievements or our accolades. We place value in the things around us based on what they cost or what they can do for us. We seek the praise of others. We begin to worry that we aren't good enough or smart enough or rich enough or beautiful enough. We forget who we are and to whom we belong. Our dreams die and our spirits wither. Hope fades and grace is forgotten. It's not that the world has changed; it's that we have wandered far from the world God first called into being and pronounced good. If we could only see the world the way God sees it, then we would know its value. If we could only see ourselves as God sees us, we would see Children of infinite worth. If we could only rejoice in the promise of life abundant, then our hearts would be full and our spirits would dance. Sometimes we have to travel a long way to discover we are already dwelling in paradise.

'Postle Jack 'Tends a Wedding
John 2:1-10

"On the third day there was a wedding in Cana of Galilee, and the mother of Jesus was there. Jesus and his disciples had also been invited to the wedding. When the wine gave out, the mother of Jesus said to him, 'They have no wine.'…Now standing there were six stone water jars,…each holding twenty or thirty gallons. Jesus said to them, 'Fill the jars with water.' And they filled them up to the brim. He said to them, 'Now draw some out, and take it to the chief steward.' So they took it. When the steward tasted the water that had become wine, and did not know where it came from…, the steward called the bridegroom and said to him, 'Everyone serves the good wine first, and then the inferior wine after the guests have become drunk. But you have kept the good wine until now.'"

Once when I was in college I heard a preacher start a sermon like this: "If you don't like a party, you won't like heaven!" Well, that certainly got my attention, and I listened to the rest of what he had to say. Years later, I have forgotten his exposition of the text and his elaboration of that statement, yet I still remember his opening line!

God must like celebrations, because Jesus seems to be at lots of them, and the Bible seems to be filled with them. So, I imagine that heaven might very well be much like a party, and a wedding party at that. Of course, the wedding party is merely that: a party. What makes all the difference is how people live their lives after the party is over. If we really have entered into a new way of life, and that new way of life is characterized by the joyful presence of God, then wouldn't it make sense that the party would continue well into eternity. After all, what other response would there be to God's joyful presence than a celebration with the best wine and the best music and the company of friends and family? It's not sacrilegious to imagine heaven is like a party. What is sacrilegious is to live our lives as if God's presence in it doesn't bring us any joy. What is unforgivable is to imagine that eternity would be spent in some way other than in celebration.

If heaven is really like a party, shouldn't we already be celebrating, every day of our new lives?

———⇒♦⇐———

'Postle Jack Wears a Path
Luke 13:6-9

Then Jesus told this parable: "A man had a fig tree planted in his vineyard; and he came looking for fruit on it and found none. So he said to the gardener, 'See here! For three years I have come looking for fruit on this fig tree, and still I find none. Cut it down! Why should it be wasting the soil?' He replied, 'Sir, let it alone for one more year, until I dig around it and put manure on it. If it bears fruit next year, well and good; but if not, you can cut it down.'"

Being a Christian in Europe back in the Middle Ages was different from being a Christian in America today. Back then people didn't have the advantage of Sunday School classes to teach them the Bible stories. When they went to church on Sunday morning, the service was all in Latin, which most of them couldn't understand, so that didn't help them explore their faith. They didn't read or have copies of Bibles with study helps that they could use for their daily devotions. They didn't have all the opportunities for spiritual growth we have available to us today.

Instead, they developed other kinds of practices for spiritual growth. They had prayer services every day. They had lots of music in worship services. They had stained glass windows that portrayed the great Bible stories: Moses parting the Red Sea, Jesus raising Lazarus from the tomb, Jesus welcoming the children. One spiritual discipline that was developed during that time was the walking of the labyrinth. The labyrinth was an elaborate twisting path, laid out with rocks or through a garden. A person would start at the beginning and walk slowly and meditatively along the path. It would wind its way into the center of a great circle, and at each turn, the walker would stop and pray for whatever it was they were concerned about. Then, when you got to the middle of the circle, you would turn and work your way back out. Over the centuries, various monasteries developed different designs for their labyrinths and many of them became world-renowned. Pilgrims would travel from all over Europe to walk these famous labyrinths; it was a way of nurturing their own spiritual journey into the sacred realm of God's holy presence.

Labyrinths have made a comeback in recent years. They seem to be everywhere: at church camps, at national conferences, even in the multipurpose wings of some churches. Walking a labyrinth is just one opportunity we modern Western Christians have for intellectual, emotional, and spiritual growth in discipleship. We can attend worship in a language we understand. We can study the Bible by ourselves and with others in groups or classes. We can turn on the television or the radio and be inspired or instructed. There are all sorts of ways we can grow in our faith.

But that growth doesn't just happen. It requires energy and effort on our part to engage in the spiritual disciplines and opportunities available to us. It requires attending to your personal spiritual growth and discerning your path in life, where God is leading you and how you might more fully walk in God's way.

If we don't walk the path, then we aren't trying to find the way. Sometimes it helps to have someone start you on the path, and show you the way to walk. And sometimes it helps to have someone to walk with you, a companion along the way.

———⟫●⟪———

'Postle Jack Sets A Light
Matthew 5:14-16

Jesus taught them, saying: "You are the light of the world. A city built on a hill cannot be hid. No one after lighting a lamp puts it under the bushel basket, but on the lampstand, and it gives light to all in the house. In the same way, let your light shine before others, so that they may see your good works and give glory to your Father in heaven."

Why church? It's a question I've been asking for quite some time now. I don't mean, "Why do we have church buildings?" I mean, "Why do we gather together as congregations? Why do we form denominations and churches?" Can't I shine brightly as I go about my day, being kind to neighbors, praying for my enemies, offering my resources of help and hope to those in need? Well, sure I can, and I should. That would be pleasing to God. But the things Jesus said and the things Jesus did were all done in public. Jesus's words weren't spoken to individuals; they were spoken to crowds. The "you" is plural; the task is singular. When we come together as a community of faith we are able to be salt and city and light. When we come together as a particular manifestation of the larger community of believers across the face of the globe God's light shines through us and becomes a beacon of hope and salvation to those who walk in darkness.

Why Church? It's not so we can have a great place to worship and feel good about ourselves. It's so we can be more clearly that visible grace of God present in the world, like a lantern lit and set upon a lampstand, giving light to all who gather around it.

Printed in the United States
29788LVS00001B/490-492

9 781931 195669